The Thunderbolt's Jest

A Detective Story

By
JOHNSTON McCULLEY

WILDSIDE PRESS

CONTENTS

CONTENTS

THE THUNDERBOLT'S JEST

CHAPTER I

SOME PECULIAR THINGS

SAGGS came to a sudden stop beside the long table in the center of the big living room, rubbing his hands together nervously, licking at his dry lips, glancing furtively here and there around the apartment like a fugitive from justice, afraid of the sudden sight of an officer of the law.

As to personal appearance and stage presence, Saggs did not rate highly. Saggs was far from being of the Greek-god type, and he knew it and gloried in his great ugliness, which consisted of a bullet-shaped head, protruding ears, tiny eyes that glittered, a low brow, thick lips, and other facial characteristics that gave him the appearance of a vicious thug. Saggs was a valet, not a thug, though in the dim and distant past he had done several little things that were not strictly within the law.

The present agitation of Saggs was due more to nervousness than to fear, however, and what little fear he did feel was not for himself alone. Now he made certain that the shades were drawn at all the windows, snapped on another light above the table, walked nervously to the hall door and back again, and stood listening to the sounds from an adjoining room.

He heard a merry, though subdued, whistle, and then a popular song hummed lightly. Presently there came to him the sounds of quick steps, a door was opened, and John Flatchley, in full and correct evening dress, stepped briskly across the big living room to the table in the center.

"I shall leave in a moment, Saggs," he said.

"Yes, sir."

"You ordered the closed car?"

"It is waiting, sir."

"My gloves!"

"Yes, sir!"

Saggs was the valet now, and he hurried to do as he had been commanded. His nervousness had disappeared seemingly in the presence of John Flatchley, his employer. Give Saggs a thing to do, and he centered his mind on it and did not let other things bother him for the time being. Saggs possessed what John Flatchley called a single-track mind.

He returned with the gloves, and watched Flatchley as though in keen expectation. Flatchley sat down beside the table, plucked at his upper lip for a moment, smiled, sighed, and suddenly glanced up at his valet with a peculiar expression on his face.

"Saggs!"

"Sir?" Saggs asked, taking a step nearer the table and watching his employer closely.

"Do you see anything wrong with me, Saggs?"

"Nothing at all, sir."

"You don't see a change of any sort going on in me—at this very moment? Nevertheless, Saggs, there is a change taking place. Watch closely, Saggs. Ah! I have changed. I no longer am John Flatchley. I now am The Thunderbolt!"

"Yes, sir." Saggs gulped, and then he grinned suddenly and stepped nearer the table. "Gosh, boss," he added, "I didn't know whether you was goin' to do that changin' stunt again before you left the apartment. I sure wanted you to do it."

"So that you might have the opportunity, I take it, to murder the poor old English language once more," John Flatchley said. "Why did you want me to change?"

"Because I've been thinkin' things over, boss, and I feel like talkin'."

"Thinking over things is an estimable thing to do, Saggs. The man who stops to think things over occasionally is a wise man. But sometimes talking is neither estimable nor wise."

"Boss, this thing to-night seems to me to be takin' some mighty big chances," Saggs blurted out suddenly. "If the least little thing goes wrong we——"

"Do you wish me to understand, Saggs, that you are afraid?" The Thunderbolt demanded.

Saggs' face turned almost purple.

"Aw, boss, you know that I ain't afraid for my-self," he replied. "I ain't carin' much what be-comes of me. But it's different with you, boss—and it's you that I'm worryin' about."

"Your solicitude pleases me," The Thunderbolt observed.

"Make talk that I can understand, boss—please," Saggs begged. "You haven't forgotten about that Radner man, have you? He's bad medicine."

"You are speaking, I take it, of Detective Martin Radner of our city police force. No, Saggs, I haven't forgotten Detective Radner. Once seen closely, Detective Martin Radner is a man never to be forgotten."

"He's a smooth one, boss, and he's sure on your trail," Saggs said.

"I believe that he has been on my trail for some weeks—and a lot of good it has done him," The Thunderbolt replied. "Saggs, I intend going ahead with my work, though a thousand Martin Radners suspect me. His suspicion only causes me a little extra trouble, that is all—and keeps me more alert. It is an excellent thing in its way. And perhaps after to-night's affair he will be ready to decide that his suspicions are unfounded."

"I sure hope so, boss."

"The trouble with you, Saggs, is that you do not know all my plans, and you feel a bit timid about our little enterprise. I have told you only that part in which you will have a share. And I want to warn you once more, Saggs, that the slightest mistake to-night on your part might cause disaster for me."

"I won't make any mistake, boss."

"Let us hope not. You are sure that you can remember all your instructions?"

"I've got everything down pat, boss," Saggs answered. "But it makes me feel shivery."

"Why?"

"Oh, it ain't the first part of the work, at all, boss. That's hard and dangerous, but I ain't afraid of cops and dicks to any great extent; but if it happens that I've got to mix up with them society folks——"

"Saggs, I belong to their crowd, and you 'mix up' with me every day, don't you?"

"But you're human, boss, and some of them look like they ain't," Saggs declared.

"Forget them. Simply do your work when the proper time comes," The Thunderbolt instructed. "You'd better start about fifteen or twenty minutes after I leave, Saggs."

"Yes, sir."

"You are sure that you remember everything?"

"Quite sure, boss."

"And you'll have to move fast, remember. And remember also the signals we agreed on, and for Heaven's sake don't be in too big a rush at the crucial moment, just because there happen to be a few persons in evening dress around."

"I won't, boss."

"Very good! We must let nothing happen to spoil it, you know. After to-night we'll have two more little enterprises, and then I think we can retire from a life of crime. Well, Saggs, I'd better be going. Watch me closely. I am no longer The Thunderbolt—now I am John Flatchley."

"Yes, sir." Saggs gulped again.

He crossed the room quickly and went through the little hall to the door and held it open, and John Flatchley, laughing a bit, stepped into the corridor and went toward the elevator.

Saggs locked the door, snapped off some of the lights, and reëntered the living room. He lighted a cigarette, sat down beside the table, and puffed a cloud of smoke toward the ceiling like a man trying to soothe his nerves.

For fifteen minutes he sat so, and then, glancing at the little clock on the mantel, he got up quickly and hurried into his own room. He removed the suit he was wearing and substituted a similar one that was a bit older and much worn. He put on a cap, snapped out more of the lights in the suite, listened for a moment at the hall door, and then opened it and slipped out.

Saggs made his way rapidly to the back of the building and the rear stairs. Down these he went, swiftly and almost silently hanging back now and then to avoid being seen and recognized by other persons going up and down.

He came finally to the exit, a door that opened into the alley back of the apartment house, darted outside, and walked rapidly through the alley to the nearest street, keeping in the deep shadows as much as possible.

Turning up the street, Saggs walked to the middle of the next block and went into a dark alley there, careful that he was not being observed. He came to an old shed, stood in the darkness at the end of it for a moment, listening, and then, certain that there was nobody near, he kicked away a pile of trash that had been against the shed's foundation, reached down into a hole that had been covered cunningly, and pulled out a small bundle wrapped in back cloth.

With this bundle under his arm Saggs went out to the street and turned up it again. He crossed a wide boulevard with traffic and found himself in a district of mansions and homes of the wealthy, yet only four blocks from the bachelor apartment house where John Flatchley had his suite.

Saggs walked along the street now like any honest pedestrian attending strictly to his own business. The bundle he carried scarcely could be seen because of the black cloth in which it was wrapped. But Saggs was alert, cautious; he felt a bit of fear.

Disaster would follow if some policeman were to stop him and make an examination of that bundle, for it contained the peculiar hood and mask worn by The Thunderbolt, also his gloves, a coat, and a pair of trousers of thin black material constructed to be donned over other clothing, together with an automatic pistol and an electric torch.

When Saggs was still a block and a half from his destination, the splendid new mansion of William Brailson, which was to be opened to-night with a brilliant social affair at which John Flatchley would be a guest, he already could see automobiles arriving and dropping guests. The big house was ablaze with light; there were scores of persons on the wide veranda and the front lawn, and the strains of an orchestra could be heard.

Saggs was well aware of the fact that he had a difficult rôle to play and that the next few minutes would be fraught with danger. He had orders from The Thunderbolt to get inside that house unobserved and in a peculiar manner. The success of The Thunderbolt's plans for the night depended on it. And Saggs knew that he faced no easy task, for the place was swarming with members of the police force and special officers.

William Brailson, the host, knowing that his guests would be dressed richly for this occasion and that the ladies would try to outdo one another in the exhibition of jewels, had taken steps to see them protected.

At his request, officers had been detailed to scatter around the neighborhood and watch for suspicious characters. The wide lawn was dotted here and there with detectives who mingled with the guests. Inside the house there were more officers, under the personal command of Detective Martin Radner, the clever member of the department who had sworn to capture The Thunderbolt.

Saggs realized that he might be stopped at any moment, and, did the officer who stopped him happen to be suspicious, that incriminating bundle beneath his arm would be investigated. The Thunderbolt's hood would be recognized and Saggs would be questioned. He did not hope that he could, in such event, make them think that he was The Thunderbolt himself. An investigation would lead to his employer, John Flatchley, who already had been under suspicion.

But Saggs dared not think of Flatchley being arrested for The Thunderbolt's offenses. It would mean a loss of social standing for Flatchley, and undoubtedly a term in prison, black disgrace for life. And Saggs, who knew and appreciated John Flatchley's motive in being The Thunderbolt on occasion, felt that he did not deserve such a fate.

It remained, then, for Saggs to get into the Brailson house safely, without being recognized, without that bundle falling into the hands of the police. For if the slightest suspicion was aroused The Thunderbolt could not do his work.

Even as he worried about doing his appointed part, Saggs chuckled at the plan as he knew of it, a sort of double plan whereby The Thunderbolt hoped to add another victim to his list and at the same time allay the suspicions of Detective Martin Radner.

"Some scheme!" he muttered to himself now.

Then he forgot it for the time being and became more alert, knowing that he was in the enemy's country, in a manner of speaking. He had reached the edge of the Brailson lawn without trouble, but the space from here on the path was fraught with danger.

So far as Saggs knew, every tree might have a man behind it, an officer of the law ready to give chase or ask questions. And it seemed almost impossible to get into that house without being seen, when the big, new mansion was ablaze with light, with lights strung around the veranda and from tree to tree across the driveway.

"Has to be done," Saggs told himself. "The boss depends on me doin' it."

He tucked the black bundle more lightly beneath his arm, wishing that he could make it smaller, left the sidewalk, then darted to the nearest clump of bushes. Saggs blessed the Brailson gardener for having decided that the lawn needed a clump of bushes just there.

Saggs crouched there in the shadows, glancing across the lawn, trying to ascertain where the officers were located. He was not worrying yet about the detectives and plain-clothes men who mingled with the guests; what worried him was the possibility of a uniformed man resting quietly against the bole of a tree, ready to observe any shadow that darted across the lawn.

"Have to be goin' on," Saggs warned himself. "Can't camp around here."

He left the protection of the deep shadows and darted quickly to another dark patch. Perhaps good fortune would be with him, he thought. As far as he could see, there was no policeman loitering around in the vicinity.

Once more he made a quick dash, and once more he came to rest in the deep shadows. And now, from a few feet distant, came an imperative, harsh voice:

"Hey, you! What's the big idea? Who are you, and where do you think you're goin'?"

The loyal heart of Mr. Saggs seemed to cease beating for the moment. A ball of fire seemed to be in his throat, choking him. Flashes of color passed before his eyes, as though he had bumped his head and received a hard shock.

His eyes pierced the darkness whence came the

harsh voice, and Saggs saw a dark figure walking slowly toward him, and saw something more—the play of light on the barrel of a weapon.

Saggs knew in that instant that there was but one thing to do—make a run for it. Things were bad enough since he had attracted some attention, but if he could get away without being seen so as to be identified later, it might not be so bad. The police would think he had been just some ordinary prowler or sneak thief who had been hiding there and surveying the scene.

"Come here out of that!" the policeman was commanding, still walking forward. "Come out of there quick, or we'll have a little target practice!"

Saggs suddenly flattened himself against a tree and circled it, peering around the side of it like a squirrel. The officer came forward with a rush, growling threats and commands.

Quickly Saggs darted away in the opposite direction, hoping and praying that everything would be all right, yet fearing to hear the roar of a revolver and to feel a sudden thud in his body that would mean a bad wound.

He reached the next dark patch in safety and sped on. Then the roar of the revolver came, but Saggs did not feel so much fear now. He knew that the policeman behind him was not shooting to make a hit, but was firing into the air to frighten and to sound an alarm. For wise Mr. Saggs, after reaching that first dark spot, had started running straight toward the house, straight toward the groups of guests, and a wild bullet might mean the death or serious injury of one of Brailson's friends.

Soon Saggs came to the edge of the driveway, where there were lines of trees, borders of bushes, and banks of foliage. He heard shouts being exchanged, heard other officers running. Crouching in the darkness, Saggs ascertained that they had lost him for the moment, for they all were bearing away to the left.

Saggs did not hesitate now. He knew that a methodical search of the grounds would begin at once, unless the other officers were convinced that the one who had given the alarm had seen nothing but a shadow. And a methodical search might result in his capture.

Hurrying along the driveway, keeping close to the bushes, making not the slightest noise, Saggs, with the precious and dangerous bundle still held beneath his arm, came to one of the rear corners of the big house.

He knew his ground well now, for it had been explained to him in detail by The Thunderbolt, who had illustrated his explanations with a comprehensive map. In the basement wall was a little square swinging window, just as The Thunderbolt had said there would be.

Saggs swung the window open quickly and slipped

inside like a shadow, closing the window after him silently and carefully. He was in pitch darkness now, but he was not at all worried by that. He stopped for an instant and then put all thought of the pursuit out of his head and concentrated his mind on carrying out to the last detail The Thunderbolt's commands.

William Brailson undoubtedly would have been greatly surprised to learn that Mr. Saggs knew more about this new mansion than did the owner himself. And he undoubtedly would have been even more surprised to learn that the knowledge had been imparted to Saggs by John Flatchley. Yet such was the case.

Saggs, holding one hand out before him to encounter any furniture that might be in that dark basement room, crossed to the opposite wall and felt around it until he located the latch of a door.

He opened the door, listened for a time, and then crept along a dark hallway. Now he was forced to grope around again, until he found the mouth of a ventilating shaft that ran up into the house. The door of the shaft was easily opened, and Saggs crept inside and closed it again, but he did not catch the latch.

Now he had the most difficult part of his work before him. Up the sloping shaft he was forced to go. The heat was stifling; dust seemed to be everywhere.   Saggs soon felt the perspiration trickling from his face and neck and arms.

He tried to estimate the number of feet that he had crawled through the ventilating shaft, and finally he came to a stop, took the flash light from the bundle beneath his arm, and flashed it around him. Once more, he found, The Thunderbolt had given him information correct in every detail. On the floor of the ventilating shaft was a series of square metal plates.

Saggs flashed the electric torch again and counted these plates. Having located the fourth from the end of the row, he put down the bundle, propped the flash light in such a fashion that the streak of light would play across the metal plate, and from the inside pocket of his coat took a small wrench.

The plate was about two feet square and was held in place by four heavy bolts. Saggs adjusted the wrench and quickly loosened the nuts on the four bolts. Then he sat back, snapped out the light, wiped the perspiration from his face and hands, and prepared to wait. A glow of satisfaction thrilled him. So far, his part of the evening's enterprise had been attended by success.

CHAPTER II

SAGGS WAITS

IT was at Detective Martin Radner's special request that he was assigned to the Brailson residence for the evening's affair; an indulgent superior officer had given him the assignment.

"Going in for society, Radner?" he wanted to know. "Playing the open-face clothes, and all that sort of thing?"

"Only to this extent, chief—young Mr. John Flatchley is going to be a guest there to-night. He has been a particular friend of Brailson for years."

"So you are still keeping your eyes on John Flatchley, are you?" the chief asked. "Are you still of the opinion that Flatchley is The Thunderbolt?"

"I'll be blamed if I know, chief. Sometimes I think that he is The Thunderbolt, and possibly ten minutes later I tell myself that I am an ass to believe it."

"You are, Radner," his superior declared. "And I'll be blessed if I can understand how you ever happened to get on that wild and crooked trail in the first place. Young John Flatchley is the sole remaining member of a family of wealth and social prestige. He may not be so rich as some we know, but he has all the money that an ordinary young man can need, and then some. So, why should be turn crook?"

"Why does anybody turn crook?" Detective Radner snappily asked. "He had a reason, the way I look at it."

"Very well. Let us have your latest theory on the subject. It may be interesting."

"But it happens to be my same old theory, chief," Detective Martin Radner answered. "John Flatchley is an athlete and has a love for adventure and excitement. He was a member of a north pole expedition, he has hunted big game in Africa and South America, and since then he has gone in for aviation and made a name for himself."

"Oh, I know all about those things," the chief replied. "But does it follow that because a man is a real fellow like that he must turn crook?"

"There was but one other Flatchley, if you remember—an uncle. And while young John was away abroad, his uncle got into a combination with the gang of financiers well and unfavorably known as The Big Six, and they cleaned up surprisingly."

"They always do," the chief said disconsolately. He had always wanted a lot of money and never had much.

"When John Flatchley returned home his uncle was dead. Young Flatchley came in for the estate, of course, being the only remaining relative. And that estate, he found, was a great deal larger than he had expected."

"Must have shocked him," the chief commented.

"As a matter of fact, it did shock him, for his uncle had been a notoriously bad financier. So young Flatchley began investigating and found that the greater part of the estate was due to the last deal of his uncle with The Big Six. He investigated that deal, and then he made the announcement that it had been a barefaced swindle, though within the law. John Flatchley paid to the victims the money his uncle had left him, and suggested that the members of The Big Six finish the work of repaying."

"As if that gang ever let go of anything they once got their hands on," said the chief.

"They refused, of course. And then John Flatchley threatened to make them do it. He swore that before he was done every cent would be paid back to the dupes. Because, he gave them to understand, it was a stain on his family honor because his uncle had been associated with them. They expected him to rush into court with a dozen suits at law, but he did nothing of the sort. As far as they could ascertain, he made no move whatever. But about this time The Thunderbolt appeared, and we began having our hands full. Now let me call your attention to one significant fact—The Thunderbolt has robbed three men, and all three of them are members of The Big Six."

"Um!" the chief grunted.

"Conner Bradford, Cyrus G. Grantburg, and James Zamlen—all members of The Big Six. And I'm almost willing to wager a month's salary that the next man The Thunderbolt robs will be a member of The Big Six. Doesn't it look significant?"

"Any smooth crook, wishing to make a few rich hauls, would pick on The Big Six, since they happen to be the wealthiest men in our fair city," the chief informed him.

"Oh, I grant you that much," Detective Martin Radner replied. "But to me it appears John Flatchley is merely collecting from The Big Six the funds they refused to pay back, and is sending the money back to the victims himself. He thinks he is removing the stain from the family honor."

"But why do it in such a way?"

"He probably knows that he cannot touch them through the courts. Those fellows work inside the law, you know. This thing would appeal to his sense of justice and his love for adventure."

"And yet——"

"And yet," said Detective Radner, "at the time Zamlen was robbed, I felt mighty sure John Flatchley was in his rooms, and at the same moment I was holding a sort of wrestling match with The Thunderbolt a dozen blocks away."

"There you are," said the chief. "That should show you that John Flatchley is not The Thunderbolt."

"I am not quite sure yet, chief. He is a mighty clever young man, as it happens. There is just a possibility that he has fooled me in some manner. And there is another possibility—that John Flatchley is not The Thunderbolt himself, but that he is hiring The Thunderbolt to do this work."

"A man able to pull off those stunts wouldn't work for anybody except himself," the chief declared. "He'd not have to, if you ask me. Crook he is, but this Thunderbolt has courage and skill; I'll say that much for him."

"And there you are," Radner declared.

"Well, Radner, go ahead and watch John Flatchley, if it pleases you. But I'd watch around elsewhere, too, if I were you. If The Thunderbolt pulls off another big trick, we are going to hear considerable about it. That gang of financial crooks known as The Big Six has some political influence in these parts—and I don't want to go looking for a new job at my age."

So Detective Martin Radner went to the Brailson residence that evening to command the men on guard there and to keep an eye on John Flatchley. Brailson was not a member of The Big Six, and Radner did not anticipate that he would be robbed by The Thunderbolt. But the detective knew from experience that sometimes the slightest word or action will put a man on the right trail, and had hopes that by watching Flatchley he might overhear that word or see that action.

Could he have seen John Flatchley now, he would not have been at all suspicious. Flatchley had driven in his limousine to the residence of Miss Agnes Larimer, a young lady of social standing, to whom John Flatchley was betrothed. He was to escort Miss Larimer and her aunt to the Brailson affair.

He had a moment alone with the girl while they waited for her aunt to be ready. Agnes Larimer, long before, had discovered that John Flatchley was The Thunderbolt, and she approved his course. But she realized, too, the dangers that he ran—knew that, no matter what his motives or intentions, in the eyes of the law he was a thief and a burglar, and nothing more.

John Flatchley had been very careful to keep an official announcement of their engagement from becoming public, for, if disaster came, he did not want Agnes Larimer mixed up in it. She would have been willing to run the risk, but John Flatchley would not have it so.

And on this evening, while they waited for her aunt, they sat close together and spoke in whispers.

"You intend doing something to-night, John?" she asked.

"My dear girl, it were better if you did not know

my intentions," he replied. "In such case, you could say truthfully that you knew nothing. But I will say this much—it is going to be to-night."

"Oh, John, at times I am so afraid for you! Not at the Brailson house, surely?"

"Not exactly at the Brailson house, my dear. I have to take part in the society circus there to-night, as you know, and shall have to mix my own work with the pleasure."

"I don't want to know the details of your plans, of course," she said, "but do promise me to be very careful."

"You may be sure of that. I have too much to lose if I get careless."

Agnes' aunt joined them then, and they went out to the car and were driven to the Brailson house.

The new mansion was a splendid affair, and John Flatchley had a keen interest in it. He had been a particular friend of Brailson's for years, and had been best man at Brailson's wedding. This was the house Brailson had built for his bride.

John Flatchley had studied architecture, and though he did not practice the profession, it was well known that he perhaps would have made a reputation for himself had he done so. And so Brailson had called him in consultation while the new house was being planned, and Flatchley, with his eye to the future, had made several suggestions. That is why he knew some things about the new residence that its owner did not know.

When they arrived at the Brailson place, the greater part of the guests already were there. Coming down the grand staircase from the smoking room, John Flatchley stopped to greet friends and acquaintances of both sexes. And at the bottom he came face to face with Detective Martin Radner.

The men knew each other well. Flatchley realized, and had for some time, that he was under suspicion, and Radner guessed that John Flatchley knew it. But what the detective could not decide was whether John Flatchley was having sport with him or really was guilty and consequently a bit nervous.

"So you are doing society this evening?" Flatchley said.

"Business," Radner replied. "We don't want jewel thieves to get away with anything, you know. Suppose The Thunderbolt was to take a notion to conduct a raid here?"

"It probably would be profitable for him," Flatchley said. "I can see about a million dollars' worth of jewels from where I am standing."

"But it probably would prove unprofitable for him in other ways," said Detective Radner.

"I beg your pardon. You are here, of course. Perhaps The Thunderbolt will be too wise to strike while you are around."

"He hasn't been very active lately," Radner observed, watching Flatchley closely.

"Perhaps he is taking time to spend a part of what he got in his last haul," Flatchley suggested. "You had a little experience with him then, I believe."

"I did. We had a wrestling match, and I admit freely that I came out second best and that The Thunderbolt escaped me easily. But there may come another time. And that wrestling match was not all defeat for me, either. I almost made sure of The Thunderbolt's identity."

"That is interesting," Flatchley said, chuckling a bit and looking out over the gathering. "But you did not make quite sure, I take it, since there has been no arrest."

"I'm liable to make sure at any moment," Detective Martin Radner said with a trace of anger in his voice. "And when I do make sure and make an arrest, there'll be some sensation in our little village."

"Sensation is one of the spices of life," Flatchley remarked to nobody in particular. "For your own sake, Radner, and for the sake of your professional reputation, be sure that this Thunderbolt does not pull off a startling crime right under your nose."

"Let him try it!" Radner exclaimed. "Let the crook try it, and see how far he gets."

Feeling that he was losing his temper, and having common sense enough to know it was the last thing he should do under the circumstances, Detective Radner bowed and moved along the hall. But, a short distance away, he took up a position from which he could watch John Flatchley continually.

Flatchley did not seem to care whether he was under surveillance. He danced with Agnes Larimer, and then with others, and spent a time in the smoking room talking with friends. And all the time Detective Martin Radner watched.

And all the time Saggs waited in the narrow ventilating shaft, the perspiration pouring from him, waited for a certain signal that would mean it was time to get to work again.

CHAPTER III

THE HANDCUFF KING

BRAILSON had arranged as a part of the evening's entertainment a society circus. A part of it was to be held outside the house, and a part inside. The long, narrow library had been set aside for a sort of side show, and there were gathered freaks that provoked volumes of laughter from the guests.

It was a riotous burlesque, with one of the most popular young men in the city acting as general manager and ballyhoo artist. He discoursed eloquently and at length on the charms of a society fat lady, a living skeleton, a tattooed man, and a snake charmer. And finally he came to a stop before another tiny platform upon which stood John Flatchley in regular evening dress.

"Ladies and gentlemen!" the manager shouted. "Here we have the great Vadooski, the handcuff king. This evening he will give us an exhibition of his marvelous powers. Señor Vadooski!"

Flatchley made an elaborate bow.

"Whatever you may have thought of the other parts of the entertainment, this particular part certainly is no fake," the manager continued. "Señor Vadooski will demonstrate that bars and bolts, handcuffs and leg irons, chains and ropes cannot restrain him when he wishes to be free. Kindly give me your attention."

The announcer stepped quickly to the wall, drew back a tapestry, and disclosed a metal door.

"A new strong room of our friend and host," he explained. "It has been constructed purposely for him to use as a receptacle for those bundles of bonds and currency we know he possesses. Examine it thoroughly, ladies and gentlemen. You will note that the room is as a bank vault, nothing more and nothing less. It is lined with metal, and has fireproof strong boxes for papers and valuables.

"The room, you will notice, is eight feet square and seven feet high. There is no opening, except this one door, which is locked by means of a powerful combination lock. Up in that corner you will notice a ventilator four inches in diameter. That is something new—causes air to circulate properly and keep papers from getting aged, I believe, or something like that.

"What I wish to demonstrate is that there is no way out of this room. Señor Vadooski, properly manacled, will be put upon a chair in the vault. The big door then will be closed and locked. There he will be inside, unable to get out, an assistant unable to get in to aid him. There he will remain for some time, answering our signals by taps on the big door. And finally he will give us the proper signal, and the door will be opened—and Señor Vadooski will stand before us, his manacles removed."

He bowed, and his eloquence was rewarded by a burst of applause.

"This on the level?" Detective Radner wanted to know.

"Sir, this entire performance is on the level," the announcer told him. "It grieves and surprises me that you doubt it. All society stunts are on the level."

"I'd like to examine that room."

"The skeptical gentleman wishes to examine the room," said the announcer. "While the band plays, he may do so."

There was a gale of laughter. The guests supposed that Radner was a part of the show. The announcer believed that Radner was trying to help him with the fun-making. Radner wanted them to believe just that, but, as a matter of fact, he was not acting at all.

He stepped into the vault room and inspected it thoroughly. The walls were of metal, the ceiling was of metal, and tappings showed that there was no hollow surface. It was a magnificent strong room built into the library of a modern residence, and Detective Martin Radner was delighted with it.

Radner felt convinced that the vault was all right,

and he tried to tell himself that John Flatchley's pose as a handcuff king was merely part of a society prank. He walked over to the little platform once more.

"The gentleman announces that he is satisfied," cried the announcer.

"The man who gets out of that vault without somebody on the outside opening the door for him would be a peach," Radner declared earnestly.

"Señor Vadooski will do that little thing," the announcer said. "I do not mean that he will get out of the vault, but he will get out of any bonds and shackles you care to put upon him. Here we have chains and ropes, handcuffs and leg irons. I will ask for some disinterested gentlemen to come forward and assist me in manacling this man. We wish to show that there is no deception."

There was another burst of merriment, and Detective Martin Radner, a twinkle in his eye, sprang to the platform. He believed now that this was nothing more than a part of the show, but he saw a chance, he thought, to embarrass John Flatchley.

Radner curled his lips when he looked at the old handcuffs and irons that had been obtained for this stunt.

"Old stuff," he said. "Anybody but a fool could get out of those. And I'm here to bet that Señor Vadooski has keys in his clothes to fit every lock."

"It makes the señor nervous to submit to a

search," the announcer said quickly, and there was another gale of laughter.

Radner and the announcer put on the old cuffs and irons and locked them. Now that he was on the platform, Radner thought he might as well help along the show. He was there primarily to watch John Flatchley, and he certainly was doing that now.

"Ladies and gentlemen, allow me to explain again," the announcer said. "Señor Vadooski, bound and ironed, will be put into the vault. Then the vault will be locked securely by Mr. Brailson, the only person present who knows the combination. A man will be stationed at the door, and every five minutes he will tap upon it. Señor Vadooski will tap in response to inform us that he is all right and working to remove the irons. He informs me that some of these are very difficult, and that it may take him half an hour, during which time we shall look at the other attractions."

"Half an hour, eh?" Detective Radner said. "It'll be mighty hot and close in that vault."

"The ventilating system will take care of that," the announcer told him. "All ready now?"

"One moment, please," Detective Radner said.

He smiled and stepped forward again, and suddenly he took from his pocket his own professional handcuffs of the latest pattern, and with a quick and unexpected movement he snapped them upon John Flatchley's wrists below the ones already there.

"See if you can get those off," Detective Martin Radner said, chuckling.

Gurgles of joy came from the guests standing nearest, for they realized that John Flatchley, no matter how well he had prepared for this affair, could have no key ready in advance for these irons, Detective Radner was watching him closely, and he fancied that he saw a flash of dismay cross Flatchley's face But John Flatchley only bowed toward him and faced the others.

"Anybody else?" he wanted to know. "Ropes or chains, handcuffs or leg irons."

There was no reply other than another burst of laughter from his friends. For an instant Flatchley's eyes met those of Agnes Larimer, and it seemed to her that he was attempting to flash her some sort of message. There was a worried expression in her face, as though she suddenly feared his plans for the night would be ruined, whatever they might be. But if John Flatchley was worried about the same thing, he did not show it in his face or manner.

They conducted him to the vault, put a chair inside it, sat him on the chair, and lashed his legs to it with a fine rope.

"Please do not unlock and open the door of the vault until I give you the signal to do so," John Flatchley said, and once more his eyes met those of Agnes Larimer. "It may take me longer than I thought at first—this detective gentleman has put upon my wrists handcuffs of the very latest pattern, and they will be very difficult to remove. But I shall remove them, if given time."

They replied to him with a chorus of mock cheers, the band played, the door of the vault was closed, and William Brailson stepped forward quickly and turned the combination knob.

CHAPTER IV

AT WORK

JOHN FLATCHLEY had built the plans for this night's enterprise on seconds, and delay, however slight, might mean danger, failure, utter disaster, and ruin for life.

The intended victim of The Thunderbolt in this exploit was Wilson Camleigh, one of the notorious Big Six, an eccentric man of wealth who long had been noted for his stinginess, his cruelty, and his inhumanity. Camleigh had been one of the men to refuse to return the proceeds of the swindle, and he was one The Thunderbolt wished to give a sort of special attention.

From the day the plans were drawn for the new Brailson mansion The Thunderbolt had looked forward to this moment. Wilson Camleigh lived in an old-fashioned house in the next block, to the rear. He was not a guest at the Brailson affair, for Camleigh long before had cut himself off from society. His business associates endured him because of his power in matters financial; others admired the fortune he had accumulated; but nobody admired or respected the man himself.

The Thunderbolt knew that there was a fault in the construction of the Brailson house, but one that probably never would be discovered. It was that the ventilating shaft that ran to the basement hallway from some storerooms on the upper floor of the mansion passed directly over Brailson's vault and strong room, and that in the shaft the metal plates that formed the ceiling of the vault were exposed.

At The Thunderbolt's signal, Saggs would loosen one of the plates. He would get into the vault, help The Thunderbolt take off the shackles and irons, The Thunderbolt would don his hood and speed away to rob Wilson Camleigh, and Saggs would remain behind to tap in answer to the signals from the outside.

If The Thunderbolt could return successful and in time, Saggs would let himself out, fasten the metal plate in place, and leave the house, and The Thunderbolt would tap the signal on the door and emerge to continue the evening's fun. The alarm given, Detective Martin Radner, Flatchley hoped, would decide that Flatchley could not be The Thunderbolt, since he had been locked in the vault at the time of the Camleigh robbery.

But there must be no delay. Everything would have to be worked on a quick schedule. Flatchley realized the risks he was running, but thought the possible result worthy of them. He wanted to have his little deal with Camleigh, and he wanted to throw Detective Martin Radner off the track.

The door of the vault was closed, and he found himself in pitch blackness. He heard the combination thrown off, and quickly tapped the metal floor three times with one heel. From above came the tapping of Saggs on the metal plate in the roof of the vault.

Saggs had been waiting long for that signal, and he hailed it with joy. Sitting in the hot, stuffy ventilating shaft had not been a pleasant experience, especially since Saggs had been a prey for a thousand fears.

Now he worked frantically at the metal bolts, removed three of them entirely and put them carefully to one side, and let the plate swing and hang on the loosened fourth bolt. He peered over the opening, flashed the electric torch, looked down.

The Thunderbolt was working frantically, too, bending forward as far as he could, trying to untie the ropes that lashed his ankles to the chair, laboring slowly and painfully because of his manacled wrists.

Saggs tossed down the black bundle, slipped the electric torch into his pocket, let himself through the hole, and dropped. At once he flashed the torch again, fastened it and propped it against a wall, and bent down to aid The Thunderbolt.

"Thought you never was goin' to give me the signal, boss," Saggs said.

"We've got to make haste, Saggs," came the whispered reply. "And we may fail, at that. Radner, the fool, snapped his own handcuffs on my wrists."

"Maybe we can get 'em off, boss."

"Get the others off first. Keys in my right side pocket in the waistcoat. You've got the duplicates?"

"Sure, boss."

"Maybe I can stretch it to forty-five minutes, Saggs, but that is about all. But I've got a little scheme that will help in a pinch, and we may have to use it."

Saggs had been working swiftly all this time. The ropes were taken off first, and then the manacles. And then Saggs drew the electric torch closer and looked at the handcuffs Detective Martin Radner had snapped on The Thunderbolt's wrists.

"They're tough ones, boss," he whispered.

"No chance?"

"Always a chance, boss. I've got a dozen keys, but I'm not sure that any of them will fit. These cuffs are new."

He tried the keys rapidly and groaned after each failure. Both The Thunderbolt and Saggs realized that the precious seconds were flying. The man outside tapped on the door, and The Thunderbolt motioned for Saggs to respond with the arranged signal.

One of the handcuffs seemed to be looser than the other. The Thunderbolt tugged at it, wrenched it from side to side, not caring whether he bruised the flesh.

"Wait, boss," Saggs begged. "You'll be hurtin' yourself if you don't."

He had two keys left, and when he inserted the next in the lock he gave a little chuckle of glee. It turned, but it did not throw the lock open. But Saggs twisted it carefully, driving it down into the keyhole, and finally the first cuff snapped open.

"The other, boss," he whispered. "We'll beat 'em yet, boss—see if we don't."

More precious seconds were lost, but finally the other handcuff was snapped open. The Thunderbolt sprang to his feet and grasped the bundle Saggs had dropped to the floor. He slipped on the thin black trousers and coat, The Thunderbolt's hood and mask, with the peculiar device across it. He put the automatic into his pocket, placed the chair beneath the hole in the roof, and then whirled toward Saggs again.

"See here!" he exclaimed. "A padlock that is a dandy. And the door can be fastened on the inside, through those two little rings at the top. Snap on the lock, Saggs. If anything goes wrong, we won't be having them open the door suddenly and finding how things are. If they try it, they'll think that the combination isn't working or something of the sort. Quick, now!"

Saggs quickly adjusted the padlock and snapped it

shut, and then stepped back to the middle of the little room. The Thunderbolt had picked up the electric torch and put it into one of his pockets, and now Saggs boosted him, and he sprang toward the ceiling and grasped the sharp edge where the metal plate had been taken away.

Another instant, and The Thunderbolt was in the hot ventilating shaft—and Mr. Saggs was in pitch darkness in the vault room, sitting on the chair, listening for the signals from outside and prepared to answer them, and wishing that this particular adventure was at an end. Saggs preferred enterprises where there was no heartbreaking time limit.

Once in the ventilating shaft, The Thunderbolt did not hesitate. He descended it rapidly until he came to the little door that opened into the basement hallway. There he hesitated for a moment to listen, and then he opened the door and crept into the hall.

Across the hall he hurried, and into the little room through which Saggs had entered. He came to the outside window, and there he stopped again, and made certain that he had everything he might need, particularly the electric torch and the automatic pistol. The Thunderbolt had no intention of using a pistol as a weapon, but he knew that it always carried a great deal of persuasion.

Getting out of the Brailson house and across the lawn, and into the residence of Wilson Camleigh in the block to the rear presented the greatest difficulties. Opening the window wide and fastening it so for the time being, The Thunderbolt put out his head, made sure that there was nobody in his immediate vicinity, and crawled out.

Crouching in the darkness against the wall of the house, he watched and listened. The laughter of guests came from the lighted lawn in front, from the veranda, from inside the house. The Thunderbolt could even see a small throng of curious persons in the street in front.

He turned and looked toward the alley, and could see nothing. He slipped along the wall of the house carefully, always alert, half afraid that he would encounter some hurrying servant or some policeman patrolling the grounds.

And now he came to a place where he was obliged to dart across the lighted driveway. A moment he hesitated, and then he plunged, and in a clump of bushes on the other side stopped to see whether he had been observed and whether an alarm was to be raised.

But it was evident that nobody had seen him, and so he went on, darting from dark spot to dark spot as Saggs had done to get into the house, but always making his way toward the alley wall. He came to it, after a time, and stopped there again to listen and watch.

He realized well the danger he was running. The neighborhood swarmed with police, and a single glance by one of them at The Thunderbolt's hood would be enough to arouse them all, to cause pursuit and search. The Thunderbolt had to succeed in the shortest space of time possible, return to the house, let Saggs go, and be there as John Flatchley when the door of the vault was opened by Brailson.

Now he sprang up and caught the top of the alley wall in a place where he knew it to be smooth. He pulled himself up, waited for an instant, and then dropped to the floor of the alley. The alley was in semidarkness, but the street at either end was bright with light, and, looking in one direction, The Thunderbolt saw a patrolman walking slowly across the alley's end, swinging his club.

"If he knew I was here!" The Thunderbolt thought, and chuckled.

On the other side of the alley was a gate, and The Thunderbolt hurried through it without making the slightest noise. Now he found himself in an old-fashioned stable yard.

He was in the rear of the Camleigh house now. In that house he hoped to find his victim, the hated member of The Big Six who had swindled men and robbed women, always inside the limits of the law. And when he found him, The Thunderbolt would know what to do. He had a great deal of information about Wilson Camleigh and his residence, and knew where articles of value were kept.

On he went, until he was standing in the darkness

against the side of the Camleigh residence. The Thunderbolt knew that old house well. As a boy he had played around it with Camleigh's son, who had died a few years before. Yet he had no reluctance in robbing Wilson Camleigh. He knew that Camleigh deserved it, that his wealth should be taken in a measure and returned to the poor dupes who had invested their savings in a worthless scheme.

Crouching beneath a window at the side of the house, The Thunderbolt listened and waited for a moment. He did not fear the police much now. There remained for the present nothing except the actual visit to Wilson Camleigh. After that would come a time of stress and danger, during which The Thunderbolt would have to escape and get back into the other house—but he would consider those things when the time came, he told himself.

He raised himself cautiously and peered through the window. He saw the interior of an old-fashioned library, with its antique furniture, its hundreds of volumes of ancient books, its heavy desk and old rugs.

Beside the heavy desk sat Wilson Camleigh himself. But the financier was not alone going over financial papers, as The Thunderbolt had expected to find him. Across the desk from him sat Cyrus Grantburg, another member of The Big Six, and a man The Thunderbolt already had visited in a professional capacity.

The presence of Grantburg did not worry The Thunderbolt much, however. Grantburg feared him, and he knew it. A few weeks before he had seen Cyrus Grantburg quail with fear as he looked at The Thunderbolt's hood and heard his harsh, threatening voice.

Camleigh had but two servants, The Thunderbolt knew—a man and a woman, both old and willing to work for small wages. Wilson Camleigh came precious near to being a typical miser. As for the old house, it did not know a burglar alarm. Camleigh undoubtedly had some methods of protection, but The Thunderbolt did not anticipate any trouble on that score. Camleigh fondly believed that nobody knew there was anything of value in the house to steal.

The Thunderbolt slipped along the wall and toward the rear of the house again. He came to a window that opened into a dark storeroom, quickly snapped the catch with an instrument he took from his coat, and then ran back to the window of the library and watched. He wanted to be sure that the snapping of the window latch had not given an alarm.

Neither Wilson Camleigh nor his guest gave indication of the fact that there was anything wrong. The Thunderbolt hurried back to the other window, opened it cautiously, and climbed inside. He lowered the window again; such an act made a possible get-away more difficult, but he did not care to run the risk of having some prowling member of the police force find an open window and start an investigation.

Now he had to get from the storeroom, go through a hall, get into the front hallway, and hurry along it and to the door of the library. He might encounter one of the old servants at any moment, he knew, after leaving the storeroom.

He listened for a time at the storeroom door, and then quickly unlocked it with a key he carried. He opened it an inch at a time and peered into the hall. Nobody was in sight; a single incandescent light glowed halfway toward the front.

Into the hall he slipped and closed the door of the storeroom behind him. He went swiftly toward the front of the house, making no noise at all as he darted along the wall. He came to another door, one that he knew opened into the wider front hall of the residence, and there he stopped to listen again, for here was the greatest danger of meeting a servant.

Assured that there was nobody close, he opened the door on a crack and peered out. The wider front hall was empty of human beings, too. Halfway down it, The Thunderbolt could see the streak of light that came beneath the library door. As from a great distance he heard the muttered voices of Wilson Camleigh and his guest.

He was about to open the door wider and spring into the front hall, when the old woman servant appeared at the other end of it, coming from the living room.   The Thunderbolt watched her carefully through the crack in the door.

But she did not come toward the rear hall.   She turned into another room, one that The Thunderbolt knew led to a stairway used by the servants of the house.   She was going up to her own room, The Thunderbolt hoped.

He waited a moment, but she did not reappear. The manservant did not put in an appearance, and The Thunderbolt supposed that he was in the little anteroom at the front of the house, waiting for a call from the library.

The door was opened wider.   The Thunderbolt slipped out into the wide front hall, hesitated a moment, and then darted along it to the door of the library.   He held his automatic ready in his left hand now.   His right hand went out and grasped the knob of the door.

CHAPTER V

GLITTERING JEWELS

AFTER Wilson Camleigh and Cyrus Grantburg had eaten dinner, they had talked for some time over an approaching business deal in which they hoped to add to their fortunes. The details of the deal arranged, they began speaking of other topics, one of which was The Thunderbolt.

"He dealt with me, didn't he?" Grantburg demanded. "And I'll swear to you, Camleigh, that I can tell you nothing about him. And our two friends who were robbed by him say the same."

"Do you suppose he is John Flatchley?"

"I thought so at first, but I do not now," Grantburg replied. "It might be John Flatchley, of course. But I am more inclined to the belief that The Thunderbolt is some professional crook out for big game, and that he has picked us because we happen to be the richest men in town."

"And the police have done nothing!" Camleigh said mournfully. "We should have better police!"

"Detective Radner was sure at first that The Thunderbolt is John Flatchley, but now he is not so sure," said Grantburg.

"And are we to have no protection? Are we to sit around and let ourselves be robbed? It doesn't make a bit of difference whether The Thunderbolt is Flatchley or not. Whoever he is, the police should catch him."

"That isn't the easiest thing in the world," Grantburg said. "The Thunderbolt handled me, remember, and I'll say that he did it well. And he frightened Bradford almost to death. That voice of his, those eyes glittering through the slits in the confounded hood he wears—they are enough to frighten any man, especially when they are backed up by an automatic pistol."

"He hasn't bothered anybody for some time now," Wilson Camleigh said hopefully.

"But he may at any moment," Grantburg replied. "We needn't get the idea into our heads that The Thunderbolt is through. If he is Flatchley we know he isn't done, and if he is some regular, professional crook, the chances are that he will commit more crimes."

"And I—I may be the next victim!"

"If you are, you'll simply cough up," said Grantburg.

"He—he will have a hard time robbing me."

"He will, eh? He got me, didn't he—and when I felt sure that he could not, when I was taking precautions? The Thunderbolt seems to know everything, confound him! He knows where valuables are hidden——"

"Don't talk like that!" Camleigh begged. "I've got valuables here in my house."

"Then you'd better hope that this Thunderbolt doesn't know it, or he may come after them."

Wilson Camleigh, frankly nervous and frightened, bent forward across the desk and reached for the water jug. He felt the need of a drink of cold water. He had been worried about The Thunderbolt for some time, afraid of a visit from him.

"I feel that I'll go insane if the police do not catch the rascal," he said. "Must a man live in continual fear simply because he happens to have a bit of money, and some criminal is eager to get hold of it?"

"One of the penalties of being rich," Grantburg observed. "The Thunderbolt's visit to me cost me a pretty penny, if you'll be kind enough to remember. And all the howling I did to the mayor and the chief of police didn't get my money back for me."

"But it is monstrous that one man can do as he pleases with other men of wealth and position! What are the police for? Why do we pay taxes and license fees."

"That's a fine line of talk, but it doesn't get us anything," Cyrus Grantburg observed, chuckling a bit. "The police will catch him if they can—you may be sure of that. Detective Radner in particular

is out after The Thunderbolt. He made an ass of
Radner on a couple of occasions, and Radner hasn't
forgotten it."

"But, if the fellow was to come here some
night——"

"You'd be properly frightened."

"And I could do nothing but hand him my property?"

"That is all I was able to do. But you're worrying entirely too much. Perhaps he'll not come here.
You may escape a visit from the gentleman."

"I hope so. But, if he does visit me——"

Camleigh stopped, shuddered.

"And what will you do if he does visit you?"

The voice was not that of Cyrus Grantburg. It
came from behind them, from the door that opened
into the hall.

Both men whirled around in their chairs, their
eyes bulging, fear written unmistakably in their
faces. Cyrus Grantburg slumped back into his chair.

"The Thunderbolt!" Wilson Camleigh gasped.

"Sit perfectly still, gentlemen. Mr. Camleigh, do
not make an effort to reach that bell button unless
you are tired of robbing widows and orphans, swindling men, and handling crooked business deals in
general. As for you, Mr. Grantburg—we have met
before, and you know what to expect if you attempt
a foolish move."

"The Thunderbolt!" Camleigh gasped out again.

He did not seem capable of making any other remark just then. He looked at the intruder, terrified. He saw the flaming streak of fire on The Thunderbolt's hood, saw his eyes glittering through the two tiny slits in it—and The Thunderbolt's voice seemed to pierce him.

"Yes, The Thunderbolt! Have you been expecting a visit from me? Perhaps you have felt that you deserved one. Mr. Grantburg, kindly step to the window behind you and pull the shade down the rest of the way. It is not necessary, I believe, to warn you not to make a false move."

Grantburg got up, stepped to the window, and pulled down the shade. He was careful to return to his chair immediately, and to spread his hands on the desk before him. Though he did not care to admit it to the world, Cyrus Grantburg had been desperately afraid of The Thunderbolt since their first encounter.

"Thank you, Mr. Grantburg," The Thunderbolt said. "Now we can get down to business without fear of interruption. Let me say, in the first place, that I want no dealings with you this evening, Grantburg. We had our little session some time ago, and I do not wish to confine my activities to one man."

"You—you crook!" Grantburg exploded.

"Hard names cause no wounds, Grantburg, but they may cause anger, you know," said The Thunderbolt. "And I do not feel like being made angry this evening. Let me advise you, sir, to keep a civil tongue in your head. It will be best if that tongue is a quiet one also. You happen to be a guest here when I call. Just attend to your own business, and after I have gone you may resume your conversation with Wilson Camleigh. I presume you are plotting to rob the public again. Mr. Camleigh will need some plot to recoup his fortune when I have finished with him to-night."

"Why should you rob me?" Camleigh wanted to know.

"Because I wish money, and I know of no easier way of getting it than by robbing you."

"I—I'll have you thrown into jail!"

"Pardon me, but I haven't the time or the energy to waste in much laughter this evening."

"And what can you hope to get in my poor home?" Wilson Camleigh asked. "My furniture is not even new——"

"I am not after furniture. I do not happen to have a moving van with me," said The Thunderbolt, chuckling a bit beneath his hood. "I am not in the secondhand business. Firsthand with me, especially when it comes to money and valuables."

"But——"

"Please let us not waste any more valuable time," The Tunderbolt said. "I know all about you and your valuables, Mr. Camleigh, and it will be useless for you to indulge in falsehood or attempt violence."

"But what——"

"Silence!" The Thunderbolt commanded. He spoke in a low, tense voice that held a note of warning, a voice the tone of which was a menace in itself.

Wilson Camleigh flinched, and so did Cyrus Grantburg, who had reason to remember that tone,

The Thunderbolt glanced rapidly around the room and then stepped toward them, the automatic pistol held in readiness in his left hand. He spoke in a lower tone now.

"You have an old safe in a corner, behind a panel," The Thunderbolt said. "You will open it at once, Mr. Camleigh, while Mr. Grantburg stands beside it against the wall, his hands held over his head. And let us be quick about it, please."

Wilson Camleigh got to his feet slowly. His face was gray because of the fear he felt, but he was glowing inwardly nevertheless. So The Thunderbolt knew about that safe, did he? As he had said, it was an old safe. And in it at the present moment there was perhaps, fifty or sixty dollars in money, a few old odd coins, a few trinkets that would not be worth more than a hundred dollars to anybody. If The Thunderbolt took those things and got away, it would not be so bad.

Grantburg lost no time in getting against the wall and standing there facing it, with his hands held as high as possible above his head. In a way, Grant-

burg was glad to see Camleigh robbed, since he had
suffered at the hands of The Thunderbolt himself.

Camleigh stumbled across the room, pressed
against the panel, and it slipped back noiselessly and
exposed the face of an old-fashioned safe.

"Waste no more time!" The Thunderbolt commanded.

Wilson Camleigh knelt before the safe, braced
himself against the wall with one hand and with the
other began fumbling at the old combination knob.
His hand shook so that he scarcely could turn the
knob, but he struggled to do so.

The Thunderbolt stood back a dozen feet or so,
alert, on guard, watching both men carefully, waiting for one of them to make a hostile move. But it
seemed that he did not have anything to fear. Cyrus
Grantburg was trying to hug the wall, and Camleigh,
fumbling at the knob of the safe, certainly did not
give the impression that he was about to attempt an
attack.

Presently Camleigh swung the door of the safe
open and then staggered to one side and turned to
look at The Thunderbolt with a question in his
glance.

"Give me all the valuables," The Thunderbolt commanded.

Wilson Camleigh faced the safe again to do as he
had been ordered and to hide his glee. A visit from
The Thunderbolt was not so bad if the loot was re-

stricted to what was in the drawers of the safe. He would get as much publicity and sympathy as had Grantburg and the other two of The Big Six who had been robbed, and at a small fraction of the price.

He opened the lowest drawer and removed it, and took from it a small roll of bills, about sixty dollars in all. These he handed up, and The Thunderbolt stepped forward and grasped them and slipped them into one of his pockets.

Camleigh opened the second drawer, removed it, displayed it so The Thunderbolt would see easily what was in it, removed a handful of old coins not worth much, and handed them up.

"Never mind about that junk," The Thunderbolt said. "It isn't worth carrying away from the house, and you know it. Open that other drawer."

Camleigh did so, using a key for the purpose. There were a few old jewels, worth nothing except as keepsakes. He offered them to The Thunderbolt, who waved a hand to show that he did not consider them worth bothering about.

"That—that is all there is," Wilson Camleigh said in his thin and quivering voice.

The Thunderbolt chuckled suddenly, and the chuckle seemed to strike terror to the heart of Camleigh. It told him that he was not going to escape as easily as he had hoped and anticipated.

"I made the remark," The Thunderbolt said, "that I knew all about you and your valuables. I am quite

well aware that there is nothing more in the drawers
of the safe. But I happen to know, Mr. Camleigh,
that your old-fashioned safe has a false bottom, and
that beneath it is a new-fashioned compartment,
worked with another combination. We'll have a look
into that, please."

"There—there is nothing else——"

"At once!" The Thunderbolt said sharply.

Once more there was a menace in his voice, and
Cyrus Grantburg, still standing against the wall, this
time flinched openly and unashamed.

Camleigh turned on his knees and held out his
hands imploringly to The Thunderbolt.

"Don't rob me!" he begged. "Don't take from an
old man what he treasures."

"It wouldn't be a pity, or anything like that," The
Thunderbolt told him. "How did you get the
greater part of your wealth? How many persons
have you robbed under cover of the law, and how
many times have you laughed in scorn at them when
they begged you to be merciful? Open that secret
compartment, and do it quickly, or I may forget myself and use force!"

Again Camleigh moaned and bent before the safe.
Even Cyrus Grantburg turned his head enough to
watch. This was a great surprise to Grantburg.
He knew that his associate was tricky, cunning, and
a miser of a sort, but he had known nothing of the
secret compartment in the bottom of the safe.

Camleigh pressed a tiny button fashioned like the head of a bolt. The bottom of the safe slid forward so that it could be swung to one side. There, beneath the old bottom, was a tiny door, with a combination knob on it.

"Be quick!" The Thunderbolt commanded.

Wilson Camleigh gave a dry sob and fumbled at the knob. It seemed as though his hand was paralyzed, as though he never could work the combination. The Thunderbolt took one step forward, his attitude threatening.

"I said for you to be quick! I have no time for nonsense!"

Wilson Camleigh's fear got the better of his cupidity. He did not hesitate longer. The combination was worked, the small metal door was lifted.

The eyes of Grantburg bulged. In the compartment were half a dozen small chamois bags, such as are used to hold precious jewels. The Thunderbolt took another step forward.

"Hand them over!" he commanded.

"They'll get you in trouble! It is bad luck to steal jewels!" Camleigh exclaimed.

"In that case, you should hurry to give them to me," said The Thunderbolt, "since you and your immediate business associates are so eager to see me have bad luck."

"Not all?"

"All," said The Thunderbolt. "And my patience

is about exhausted, too. You have been delaying me entirely too much. I had hoped to end this visit without resorting to roughness, but it now appears that I cannot."

Wilson Camleigh did not hesitate longer. He handed up the little chamois bags, one at a time, like a mother parting forever from her beloved children, gasping as he did so.

"Now close the safe and come back to the table," The Thunderbolt ordered.

He stepped back himself as he spoke. Camleigh closed and locked the safe and staggered back to the chair beside the desk like a sick man.

"Sit down where you were, Mr. Grantburg. And let me thank you for showing good sense and keeping quiet."

Grantburg, without offering a reply, returned to the desk and sat down as before, placing his hands before him. The Thunderbolt stood at the other end of the desk.

"Not trusting you, Wilson Camleigh, I want to make sure that I have what I came after," The Thunderbolt said. "You see, I happened to know what even your associates did not—that for years you have been a jewel fiend, that you have turned thousands of dollars into precious stones and have kept them here in your house, in that secret compartment, so that you could take them out when it pleased you and gloat over them."

"Camleigh, you utter ass!" Cyrus Grantburg exclaimed. "I didn't know that you could be such a fool! Keeping a fortune in gems in the house!"

"My pretty jewels!" Wilson Camleigh wailed. "They represent so many good dollars. I can't live without my pretty gems. With them in the safe, I had a big part of my fortune right here where I could look at it and realize how much it meant. For years I have gathered them——"

"Rather glad that you did," The Thunderbolt observed. "Makes things easier for me. They are not difficult to carry, and they ought to be easily marketed. And now we'll take a look at them to make sure that you haven't been playing any more tricks."

He untied the chamois bags, and onto the desk he poured a glittering heap of flashing diamonds cut splendidly, but unset, gems that represented a fortune, jewels that would have delighted the heart of any lover of precious stones.

Camleigh uttered a cry and bent forward suddenly, but The Thunderbolt menaced him with the automatic, and he fell back again. And then he bent over the desk and gave the glittering stones a superficial examination, for he did not want to discover afterward that Camleigh had palmed off imitations on him.

"They seem to be all right," The Thunderbolt said calmly, as though he had been examining them for purchase instead of appropriating them without payment.

He swept them toward him and did not even stop to put them into the chamois bags again. He scooped them up and put them into a pocket of his coat, while Wilson Camleigh continued to gasp and Cyrus Grantburg's eyes bulged at what he had seen.

"I believe this is all for the present, gentlemen," The Thunderbolt said. "The evening has been a pleasant one, I assure you. Allow me to advise that you sit at this desk, exactly as you are, for ten minutes after I have gone. I have no time to go into details, but feel sure you understand me."

He bowed a mock bow and stepped backward.

"If you'll let me ransom the jewels——" Camleigh began in his whining voice.

"I am afraid it would be difficult. You see, I do not care to leave you my address," The Thunderbolt replied.

"I could advertise—arrange a meeting——"

"Then call the silly police to catch me in a trap? I think I'll handle these jewels myself. I can get more for them than you would give me in ransom money."

He bowed low again, and again he turned halfway from them. And then there came a knock at the door.

CHAPTER VI

GRIM DANGER

THE attitude of The Thunderbolt changed instantly. He darted a step to one side, his eyes swept over the two men at the desk, and then he glanced toward the door.

"Who is it?" he asked Camleigh.

"I don't know."

"No nonsense! Did either of you men signal in any way?"

"No—no!" Camleigh whispered, hoarsely and in fear. "There was no way to signal."

"This is your house, and you should know who might be knocking at the door of your library."

The knock was repeated, this time louder, and then a weak voice was heard:

"Mr. Camleigh, sir!"

"My servant," Camleigh told The Thunderbolt.

"Ask him what he wants."

Camleigh raised his voice. "What is it, Burton?" he asked. "Why are you bothering us?"

"Is everything all right, sir?"

The Thunderbolt menaced Camleigh suddenly with

the automatic, and there was no need for him to speak.

"Why, yes—everything is all right," Camleigh said. "Why do you disturb us?"

"There is an officer here, sir. He said that he was going through the alley and thought he saw a man prowling around the house. He came inside the yard, sir, and went around the building, and he found the window of the storeroom unfastened— and I am sure that I had it fastened, sir."

"That ain't all, Mr. Camleigh," spoke the rough voice of the policeman. "The catch has been pried open. Maybe you'd better let me search the house, sir."

Swiftly The Thunderbolt stepped to the desk. "Tell him to go ahead and search, and to start with the rooms on the floor above," he ordered. "Tell him that you are having a business conference——"

The frightened Camleigh, watching the glittering eyes of the man who wore the hood, did as he had been commanded. The policeman replied that he would search the remainder of the house and then return to the library, and, they could hear him telling the frightened old manservant what to do.

Fully did The Thunderbolt realize his danger. Wilson Camleigh, though half paralyzed with fear of him, was a jewel fiend, and might take a big chance in defense of his precious gems. He was the sort of man who, half frantic, might be expected to shout for help and then collapse.

The Thunderbolt was remembering that he had to get from the house and into the residence of William Brailson, that he wore the hood that would attract attention any place, and did not dare remove it. It was a time for quick and decisive action.

He did not know whether there was more than one officer, whether the policeman had left the old servant standing at the bottom of the stairs in the hall. Perhaps the storeroom window through which he had made his entrance was guarded. He ran the risk of meeting the officer in the hall, of having Camleigh call for help the instant The Thunderbolt left the room. But he had to act; he could hope to gain nothing by remaining in the library.

"Remember what I said—keep quiet for ten minutes at least after I have gone," he told Camleigh and Grantburg again. "Do not think to stop me merely because there happens to be a policeman in the house. If I have to fight my way out, I'll give you gentlemen some attention first of all."

Having voiced that threat, The Thunderbolt darted swiftly to the hall door. As he listened he watched Camleigh and Grantburg. They made not the slightest move. But The Thunderbolt sensed that they might do so at any instant.

He could not hear anybody in the hall. And he did not dare delay long, for the policeman, his search at an end on the upper floor, would be coming back. And there was another reason for haste, too—The Thunderbolt had to hurry back to the other house, get inside it, and change to John Flatchley again, get Saggs out of the vault room and have the metal plate in the roof bolted into place once more. Not until he had done that would he begin to feel safe.

Now he opened the library door a crack, turned to menace the two men at the desk again, then darted out into the hall and sped through it toward the narrow hall in the rear.

He expected to hear behind him the shouts of Wilson Camleigh, the loud calls of Cyrus Grantburg for help. But they did not come at once, for which The Thunderbolt was grateful. He hoped that the fear of the two men would keep them tongue-tied for several minutes yet, to give him the chance to get clear.

Now he was in the end of the hall, near the door that opened into the narrower hall in the rear of the house. He did not hesitate when he came to the door. He tore it open, dashed in, closed the other door behind him, and whirled to continue his headlong plunge toward the rear of the house.

A few feet from him another door was thrown open—and The Thunderbolt found himself face to face with an officer of the law!

What happened then did not take many seconds of time. The policeman could not mistake that hood with its red device across it. And The Thunderbolt knew well that this was an instant where nothing would count so much as quick action.

He hurled himself forward even as the officer shouted his surprise. He crashed against the policeman, knocked his revolver from his hand, threw him flat on the floor, and sped on.

There was no time to make an attempt to get through the storeroom now. And the window might be guarded by another officer, for all The Thunderbolt knew. So he flew through the hall, darted into the kitchen of the residence, slammed the door behind him, and ran to the one which, he knew, opened upon the little rear porch where tradesmen delivered supplies.

Behind him, the policeman was bellowing in rage and surprise, struggling to get upon his feet, trying to reach for his cap and his revolver at the same time.

Reaching the outside door, The Thunderbolt did not hesitate. With his automatic grasped firmly in his left hand, he wrenched the door open, sprang out upon the little porch, and slammed the door behind him. Here he was in darkness, but here he could not remain.

Out toward the alley he raced through the black night, keeping away from the streaks of light that came from distant arcs, hoping that he would not be tripped by some obstruction on the ground. Far behind him the rear door of the house was thrown open, and the policeman rushed out and fired into the air.

Now there was an added danger, The Thunderbolt knew. That wild shot would attract the attention of some of the officers that had been placed around the neighborhood to guard the Brailson place. And he would have to get across the alley and into the Brailson yard, across the yard and into the new Brailson residence, before he could consider himself even halfway safe.

All this time the minutes were fleeing, and The Thunderbolt knew that Saggs was sitting in the vault room, answering the tapped signals, and the guests would be waiting for the vault door to be opened, that they might see what Señor Vadooski, the great handcuff king, had done while imprisoned.

Now The Thunderbolt had reached the old-fashioned stable yard, and he let himself into it and continued toward the gate that opened into the alley. The policeman was still shouting behind him; The Thunderbolt heard a shrill whistle, and answers came from the other side of the alley.

He opened the gate and ran out, crouched for a moment in the darkness in an effort to locate his foes, and then sprang across and against the alley wall of the Brailson place. He knew that it would be a dangerous thing to make an attempt to reach the gate, and so he sprang for the top of the wall, grasped it, managed to draw himself up, and stretched there, panting.

Half a dozen officers were charging across the lawn toward the wall. They found the gate and hurried through it, flashing their electric torches, shouting, guided by the calls of their comrade at the Wilson Camleigh place. By this time both Camleigh and Grantburg were shouting the news of The Thunderbolt's visit for every one to hear.

The Thunderbolt let himself down inside the wall, and for a moment stood panting, alert, watching the shadows. Crossing that back lawn to the little window that would allow him to get into the basement was an enterprise fraught with great danger, he knew. The risk was as great as he cared to take, but he dared not hesitate.

To the nearest dark space he darted, reached it in safety, and stood waiting again. No more officers seemed to be running toward the gate in the alley wall. There did not seem to be any undue excitement on the front lawn or veranda, and The Thunderbolt judged that the shot and the cries of the policeman he had left behind had reached nobody except the few officers who had happened to be nearest.

The Thunderbolt darted to another dark spot on the lawn, and once more he paused to watch and listen. Before him was the lighted driveway across which he must go to reach the side of the house.

He might be seen there, and the hood he wore be recognized. This was to be the real danger zone.

But he could not crouch there in the darkness and speculate about it. Another policeman might wander into the vicinity, and then The Thunderbolt would be unable to cross, and might be discovered. He would have to take his chance immediately.

He braced himself for a sudden dash to the side of the house. Nobody was on the driveway in his vicinity, so far as he could see. The few guests who happened to be on the front lawn would not notice his sudden movement across the lighted space.

Finally he darted forward, sprang across and into the deeper shadows beyond. Noiselessly he hurried toward the little window, his ears strained to catch any sounds that would tell him he had been seen and that a chase had begun, but he heard nothing of the sort.

Now he crept along the wall, going as swiftly as possible, yet careful to make no noise. He reached the little window and let himself through. Into the basement room he crept, and across it to the door.

The Thunderbolt was commencing to breathe easier now. The worst of it, he believed, was past. He had but to reach the ventilating shaft and make his way up it.

Now he slipped his automatic into his pocket, made sure that the diamonds were safe, and opened the door before him. The mouth of the ventilating shaft was but a few feet away. A few seconds more, and he would be in the shaft.

"Close call," The Thunderbolt breathed to himself. "Saggs will be worried half to death, I suppose. Well, I was worried myself for a minute or so."

He darted along the hall and came to the door of the ventilating shaft. He felt for the catch and opened the door, and crept inside quickly. He was feeling a lot better now—the rest should be easy.

Up the shaft he climbed, through the stifling heat and the dust. He drew near the series of metal plates, and once again he became extra cautious. But he heard no sounds to intimate that anything had gone wrong.

Now he had reached the one open plate. He bent over it, taking the electric torch from his pocket.

"Saggs!" he whispered.

"Boss! Boss!" There was intense relief in Saggs' whisper.

The Thunderbolt flashed the torch and handed it down. Saggs took it and slid the chair beneath the hole. The Thunderbolt let himself down.

"Everything lovely," he reported in a whisper. "I got the loot, Saggs, but they almost got me. And we're not out of it. You'll have to be careful getting from the house."

"And they've been raisin' blazes here, boss," Saggs whispered. "You've been gone about fifty minutes,

I think. They've been tryin' to open the door, but that padlock held it. They're some worried—think that the combination is on the bum."

"Hurry, Saggs—help me!"

"All right, boss."

The Thunderbolt removed the thin coat and trousers and handed them to Saggs, who quickly rolled them into a bundle, together with the automatic pistol; everything except the electric torch, for which he would wait until the last moment.

The Thunderbolt surveyed himself in a small mirror Saggs handed him for the purpose. He took a towel and wiped some of the dust from his face.

Down on his knees, Saggs wiped off The Thunderbolt's shoes carefully, making sure that no moist earth remained on the soles of them.

"You've been signaling regularly?" The Thunderbolt asked.

"Sure, boss."

"Snap those handcuffs of Radner's on me again. He'll be suspicious if he thinks I was able to take them off."

Saggs obeyed swiftly.

"Now give me the key to the padlock. I'll have to take it off after you're in the shaft. That's right. Now—up with you!"

He boosted Saggs above, then handed him the flash light. Almost immediately Saggs had swung the metal plate back into place and was working to screw the bolts fast. The Thunderbolt sat down in the chair and listened. He could hear, faintly, Saggs working above. He could hear William Brailson, almost frantic, working at the combination. The signal came, and The Thunderbolt tapped on the door by way of reply.

And then there came a faint signal from Saggs, which meant that his work was done, that the plate was back in place, and that the inside of the vault room would look natural.

The Thunderbolt waited until he could hear Brailson working at the combination again; then he unlocked the padlock, removed it quickly, and slipped it into a pocket, putting the key into another. And then he sat down again, to wait, trying to look almost exhausted—a thing that was not difficult under the circumstances.

Outside the door was a sudden cry, a chorus of congratulations. The door was swung open, and John Flatchley blinked suddenly in the brilliant light as Brailson and some others dashed in at him.

"About time," John Flatchley gasped. "I'm almost—all in. That ventilating thing in the corner—it isn't much of a success."

He managed a sickly grin as they led him out into the room. A chorus of gasps greeted him, and his eyes met those of Agnes Larimer for an instant.

"Sorry," said John Flatchley. "Detective Radner's handcuffs were too much for me. Everything else—was all right."

"I was scared half to death. Something seemed to be wrong with the combination," Brailson said.

"It was like a furnace in there," Flatchley declared. "Where is Detective Radner? I want him to take off these confounded handcuffs of his."

But Detective Martin Radner seemed to be missing.

CHAPTER VII

STEEL BRACELETS

MISS AGNES LARIMER, possessing the intuition of a woman in love when danger threatens the man in the case, felt herself grow cold when John Flatchley was locked in the vault room.

She did not know whether this was an ordinary society circus stunt that John Flatchley was doing, or whether it was something more. For she had understood that John Flatchley would be The Thunderbolt for a time this night, but she did not know when, nor what he intended doing. And she knew his reckless nature, and with what sincerity he was maneuvering against the financial Big Six.

She had tried to read the look in his eyes just before the door of the vault had been closed upon him, and she read it to mean that the opening of that door was to be delayed as long as possible unless he gave the signal for it to be opened.

Along with the others, she had failed to see how a man could enter or leave the vault except by the one door. But John Flatchley, she knew well, was always doing the impossible. She told herself that she was loyal, that she thought he was doing right, though the law would say otherwise, but she confessed to herself that she would be glad when his exploits were at an end and all danger from that source over.

The door having been locked, the announcer led them to the other end of the long room and demonstrated another "freak" in such a manner that William Brailson's guests shouted their glee. The Brailson affair was a great success, and little Mrs. Brailson was entirely happy.

"I hope you'll be as happy soon, Agnes," she told Miss Larimer. "I'm quite sure that Mrs. John Flatchley will have a splendid new home."

"Possibly, but what makes you think I shall be interested?"

"My dear! You might as well announce it now. You've been in love for a couple of years, and you know it very well—and I saw how he looked at you a moment ago. It was like a man going to his doom might look at the woman he loved."

"Oh, I hope he isn't going to his doom," Agnes Larimer said. "Whoever suggested that he do such a thing?"

"Why, he suggested it himself when he was planning the stunts for the circus with William. He suggested a number of the very best and most entertaining things. And to think that detective man spoiled it by putting his own handcuffs on John! I detest the brute!"

So he had planned it himself! That was food for thought for Agnes Larimer. She felt sure that John Flatchley was up to one of his Thunderbolt affairs this very minute, but she failed to see how that could be. How could a man locked in a strong room rob anybody?

She tried to laugh and be as gay as her friends who' surrounded her, but she could not. She kept thinking of John Flatchley locked up in the vault. She glanced at Detective Martin Radner now and then, and she began to detest him, too. Radner seemed to be smirking, to be smiling in a knowing manner, as though he had prevented somebody from doing something.

Once or twice she wandered near the door of the strong room and heard the man outside tapping the signal, and taps coming from the inside that meant he was not ready for the door to be opened. Perhaps, she told herself, it was nothing more than a stunt after all, and that his real adventure as The Thunderbolt was to be later in the night, perhaps after he had escorted her and her aunt to their home and left them there.

"I'd hate to be the wife of a real criminal," she mused. "I never could endure the strain."

She seemed to sense what life meant to the women whose relatives were real criminals, who live always in fear of the mistake that will take from them the head of their household, their support, that will darken the remainder of their lives.

"I'd go insane!" she told herself. "I'll be so glad when John is finished with this work!"

The announcer had glanced at his watch, and now he was leading the throng of guests back to the door of the strong room.

"It is almost time for Señor Vadooski to show us that as a handcuff king he is the master of all," the announcer said.

"Give him time," Agnes begged, trying to laugh as she spoke. "He has the detective's handcuffs on, you know."

"And they'll stay there, lady," Detective Radner told her.

There seemed to be something ominous in the words, and she almost shuddered. There was an interruption of some sort, but it lasted for only a moment, and then the announcer turned to the door of the vault again.

"Signal him," he directed.

"I did signal him, less than two minutes ago, and he signaled back that he was not ready."

"Give him time," Agnes said again.

"Ten or fifteen years, anyway," Detective Radner responded, laughing.

She seemed to sense that Radner was watching her; she knew that he had held John Flatchley under suspicion and knew of Flatchley's interest in herself, and so she laughed the remark aside and gave her attention elsewhere.

But she was experiencing fright for all that. She could not forget how Flatchley had looked at her just before he had been locked in the vault, and she felt sure that there had been some deep meaning in his glance.

The man outside signaled again, and again there came from the interior the taps that meant John Flatchley was not ready.

"I suppose he is trying to get off those precious cuffs of yours, Radner," William Brailson said. "Why did you want to snap them on him and spoil my show?"

"There'll be no disgrace for him if he can't take them off," Radner declared. "Those cuffs were not manufactured out of tin, or made to be slipped off easily. It'd take a wizard to get out of them without having the key."

"I think we'd better open the door and have him out," Brailson said. "He has been in there for half an hour, and despite that little ventilating device it must be mighty hot."

He tapped on the door himself and again received the signal that all was not ready. But, laughing, Brailson stepped forward and reached for the combination knob. Agnes Larimer could not get to him to prevent it without making herself more conspicuous than she cared to do.

So she stepped back in the crowd and let some man talk to her, meanwhile trying to watch the door, hoping that her fears were groundless and that everything would be all right.

Brailson uttered an exclamation and whirled the knob again.

"Made some mistake," he said. "It didn't work."

"It's a wise man who knows the combination of his own safe," the announcer said. "Let us hope you haven't forgotten it. We may have to feed Flatchley soup through that ventilator, like they do entombed miners, until you can get a man from the factory to open the thing—or some professional yegg to blow it open."

"A lot you know about yeggs!" Detective Martin Radner exclaimed.

Radner was in the front of the crowd, watching everything closely. And when Brailson tried again, and failed to open the door, he grew interested.

"Perhaps you are making some slight error in the combination, sir," Radner said.

"I worked this thing half a hundred times yesterday; played with it like a child with a toy," Brailson declared. "I know that I am working the combination correctly. Funny thing!"

"A safe goes wrong now and then," Radner said.

"Quiet—you'll frighten the women!" the announcer whispered in his ear. He turned to face the others. "While our good friend and host is trying to recall the combination of his vault, allow me to show you something else interesting," he cried. "If you'll kindly follow me to this little platform——"

The greater part of the guests followed him, but some remained behind to watch Brailson at work. Brailson, the perspiration standing out on his forehead, a look of fear in his face, had worked the combination half a dozen times, and yet had been unable to open the door.

Brailson, it was evident to all, was badly worried. He did not wish the housewarming of his magnificent residence marred by an accident of this sort. He could see screaming headlines in the newspapers saying how John Flatchley was held a prisoner in the Brailson vault until an expert could open it, how society women had fainted and men had turned pale.

Now and then he tapped on the door, and always the tapping was answered from inside. That reassured him in a measure, but he wanted most of all to get the door open and rescue John Flatchley.

Detective Martin Radner had walked toward the entrance to the hallway, a little disgusted. He believed that Brailson, in his nervousness, was trying to work the combination wrong and would not take the time to calm himself before trying again.

Detective Radner walked back into the room, through it into the one adjoining, and found himself where an open French window allowed him to step out upon the veranda. There he found one of his men making frantic signals to him.

"What's wrong?" Radner demanded, stepping over to the railing.

"A shot, and a lot of shouts, coming from that place across the alley," the officer reported. "Some of the men have gone there."

Radner sprang over the railing and motioned more of his men to him.

"It may be some sort of a trick," he said. "All you others remain here and keep your eyes open. Careful, now!"

Detective Radner left them there and hurried across the lawn to the alley gate. He could hear the shouts plainly now, and heard The Thunderbolt mentioned. Radner seemed to turn cold. What if The Thunderbolt had committed another crime, and right over there? Radner remembered that the house belonged to Camleigh, one of The Big Six.

He dashed across the alley and through the other gate, collided with one of his men, and hurried with him to the house. An instant later he was inside, and a half-frantic Wilson Camleigh was shouting into his ears how he had been robbed of a fortune in diamonds.

Radner took charge immediately, posted his men, forced Camleigh and Cyrus Grantburg before him into the library, and made them tell the story as calmly as possible.

When it was done, he asked a score of questions and found that the answers meant nothing to him. The Thunderbolt had come, had taken the jewels, and had gone again in the face of an alarm.

Radner telephoned the news to headquarters. He sent out orders to make a thorough search of the neighborhood, though something seemed to tell him that it would avail nothing. And then, out in the darkness again and hurrying back to the Brailson place, he acknowledged to himself that this business disgusted him, and that unless he could do something about it soon he would resign his position before they could ask him to do so.

The Thunderbolt had come and gone, taking a fortune in jewels, while just across the alley a swarm of officers under the command of Detective Martin Radner had been guarding guests at a social gathering! Radner felt that he never could live that down.

And what about his suspicion that John Flatchley was The Thunderbolt? Was not Flatchley at that moment locked up in a vault from which there could be no escape? Or—was he?

Detective Martin Radner darted back to the Brailson place, ran quickly along the illuminated driveway, sprang over the rail of the veranda, and hurried to the library.

He found that Flatchley had just been taken from the vault and was calling for Radner to remove the handcuffs. The detective hurried toward him.

"They were too much for me, Radner," Flatchley said. "It wasn't fair to spring new stuff on me like that. Take them off, for Heaven's sake, and let me get at my handkerchief. They had one deuce of a time getting the door of that strong room open."

Radner, without replying, reached into a pocket and took out his keys. He selected the right one and reached for the handcuffs. John Flatchley extended his wrists. Radner's hands went forward to do the work required, but suddenly he stopped.

"So you didn't get them off?" he asked. "Señor Vadooski failed, did he?"

"They were much too up-to-date, I am afraid," John Flatchley said, grinning.

"I find something very peculiar here, then," Detective Martin Radner declared, his eyes widening a trifle. "You weren't unconscious in that vault, I suppose?"

"No. Why do you ask?"

"And nobody was in there with you?"

"Everybody here ought to know the answer to that," Flatchley answered.

"Nobody else could have taken off those handcuffs, then. And you say that you did not. This is what is peculiar to me—they are not on you the same way they were when I saw them last."

"Wh-what?" Flatchley gasped.

"One of those handcuffs has a peculiar nick in it, a sort of identification mark. And I noticed when I snapped them on you that the nicked handcuff went on your right wrist. Now it is on the left. Yet you say that you didn't get them off!"

CHAPTER VIII

"SOME NIGHT!"

FULLY a score of persons had heard Radner's statement, and they looked at the detective and at John Flatchley in wonder. There was a moment's silence, and then Brailson took a step forward.

"Confound it, Radner, are you trying to spoil my show?" he asked. "You lock those things on Flatchley, you swear he cannot get them off, he admits that he can't, and then you swear that he has had them off already."

"I can't deny the evidence of my eyes," Radner declared hotly. "I say those handcuffs have been taken off and put on again."

"Which is admitting that I am some handcuff king," declared Flatchley.

Flatchley had had a moment's consternation at Detective Radner's statement, but he was himself again now. He knew how it had happened, of course, and he rebuked himself for not examining the cuffs before he had removed them. But there had been so little time.

"I think you are just a bit reckless in your statements, Radner," Flatchley said now. "Of course it is absurd to tell these ladies and gentlemen that I have had the handcuffs off. Wouldn't I be the first to boast of it? You have made a mistake, that is all."

"You can't make me believe it," Radner said. "And now, Mr. Brailson, I'll have to ask your aid, please. The Thunderbolt, I am informed, has just paid a visit to your neighbor, Mr. Camleigh, who lives across the alley, and has stolen a fortune in diamonds."

"The Thunderbolt has robbed Camleigh!" a dozen exclaimed at once, looking at one another wildly.

"He has—and with a bunch of police within a block of the place," Detective Radner admitted. "One of my men declares that he thinks he saw a man running toward this house. I am going to search the rear of the house, Mr. Brailson, with your permission."

"Do so, by all means, but please annoy my guests as little as possible," Brailson replied. "Everything seems to be conspiring to spoil my entertainment this evening."

"I hope it will not be necessary to annoy the guests," Radner said.

"At least you may be sure that I did not rob Camleigh," John Flatchley said boldly and with a smile. "I'd have had a hard time doing it, locked up in that vault."

"As hard as removing those handcuffs?" Radner asked nastily.

Flatchley's face flushed, and he glanced quickly at Brailson.

"Our detective friend seems to think that I might have committed the crime myself," Flatchley said. "I insist, Radner, that you be more careful in your language. I have some friends who are not without influence around police headquarters."

Detective Radner's face turned purple at this subtle threat, and inwardly he cursed himself for having spoken and having acted as he did. It enraged him to think that John Flatchley perhaps was secretly laughing at him now.

"To demonstrate your innocence, Mr. Flatchley, I'll just inspect the vault room again," he said.

Without another word he stepped into the vault, while John Flatchley and the others watched him and smiled. Radner tapped the floor, ceiling, and walls of the vault again, fortunately for Flatchley missing the metal square that Saggs had opened. When he emerged he met Flatchley's eyes squarely.

"I suppose the idea is ridiculous," the detective admitted, "but I am still puzzled about those handcuffs."

"Just a mistake, that's all," Flatchley said soothingly. "You noticed that mark of which you speak, and believed it to be on a certain wrist. Possibly I had my wrists crossed at the time. That might account for it."

"Possibly," Radner acknowledged reluctantly.

He hurried from the library to answer a call from one of his men. John Flatchley turned into the crowd and met Agnes Larimer. Talking and laughing together, they moved out to the veranda and along it toward one end that was deserted.

"John!" she whispered. "You——"

"Little girls should not ask embarrassing questions, my dear," John Flatchley told her, laughing softly. "I do not want you to know too much, you see. Perhaps, some day, I'll be able to tell you everything."

"But how on earth could you have done it, John? You were locked in that terrible strong room."

"There is an answer, of course, but I do not want to tell it to you yet," Flatchley replied. "I may say, however, that everything went off smoothly. And we find ourselves that much nearer the end, my dear girl. Two more little enterprises, and my work will be over. And I'll be glad!"

She squeezed his hand, and, as they turned to retrace their steps, John Flatchley's arm swung away from his side. Out into the night, out across the Brailson lawn, sailed the little padlock that had protected the inside of the vault door.

Flatchley had been worrying a great deal about that padlock. He had no desire to be searched and have the lock found upon him. It might be difficult to explain, especially to Detective Martin Radner. It might cause Detective Radner to investigate along new lines, might set his mind to work in more dangerous channels. With the padlock out of his possession, John Flatchley felt considerably better.

He was wondering now, while he walked the veranda and listened to Agnes talk, what Saggs was doing, whether he had got away from the Brailson house safely and had reached home without trouble. He had not told Saggs that the stolen jewels were in a pocket of the coat in the bundle. Saggs, he knew, would get that bundle home just as it was, if possible, and hide it in a certain place where it generally was hidden when The Thunderbolt was not at work.

But Mr. Saggs had been doubting whether he ever would get home safely with the bundle. He had worked like a maniac in the ventilating shaft to fasten the metal plate back into place, and had signaled John Flatchley when he had finished, and then had rested for a moment, wiping the perspiration from his face and hands and promising himself that never would he work in such a place again.

Then, sure that the bundle was compact, and nothing would be lost, Saggs started down the shaft slowly, glad that so much of the night's adventure was over, but wishing that it was all ended.

The Thunderbolt had scored again. Saggs chuckled when he thought of that. If The Thunderbolt had got what he went after, and had returned, then The Thunderbolt was safe, Saggs believed. To catch him, they would have to catch him in the act. The Thunderbolt planned everything to the last detail. He would not be the one to leave damaging evidence behind at the scene of a crime.

Saggs came to the last turning in the ventilating shaft, and had but a few feet more to go before reaching the little door that would let him out into the basement hall.

But suddenly he came to a stop, his heart hammering at his ribs, trying to keep from breathing for the moment. There was a light burning now in that basement hall, and Saggs could hear voices.

"The boss said to search every inch of this basement," one of the voices was saying.

"Well, we have gone over it twice," declared another. "Radner himself couldn't find any more than we have found. And we haven't found anything except a couple of tracks on the floor of that laundry room across the hall. They don't mean anything, if you ask me."

"Cops!" Saggs told himself, and suddenly he snarled.

Saggs never had loved the police. In the old days before John Flatchley had met him, the police had been Saggs' natural foes, and his enmity for them was a thing bound to endure.

But he was quick to realize that this predicament

was one of danger for him. For some reason the police were searching the basement and the rear of the house. His retreat was cut off for the time being. He did not believe that they would search in the ventilating shaft, but he would be unable to leave the basement while they were there.

Then a thought came to him that brought with it a twinge of sudden fear. Did the presence of the searching officers mean danger to The Thunderbolt? Had The Thunderbolt, for the first time in his career, made some fatal error? Knowing The Thunderbolt as he did, Saggs could not believe it, yet he knew that no man is proof against mistakes, and so he feared.

He crept back up the ventilating shaft, back into the dust and the heat, the precious bundle of The Thunderbolt still beneath one arm. And there he remained, listening intently, watching for the light in the basement to go out.

Saggs did not have a watch on, but he guessed that it was growing late. He certainly would have to get out of the house before daylight, else remain in that stifling ventilating shaft throughout a day and wait for another night. The very thought of such a thing made him feel ill.

Because of his forced inaction a thousand thoughts assailed him. He began fearing again that The Thunderbolt had made some mistake, that John

Flatchley had made some error after being released from the strong room.

Saggs waited for what he thought was half an hour, and then he crept down the shaft again and approached the little door. The light in the basement was out, so far as he could see. Down to the little door he went, and unfastened the catch and opened the door a couple of inches or so.

He was glad afterward that he took the time and trouble to peer out and along the hall. His heart almost stopped beating when he did. The light in the hall had been snapped out, but far down the corridor another was burning, and in the dark hall within ten feet of the shaft door, silhouetted against the distant light, stood a patrolman.

Saggs almost cursed in his disappointment. He closed the door softly, and once more withdrew up the ventilating shaft. He could hear nothing up there, and so he wondered what was taking place, and this caused him greater anxiety.

Like many another man, Saggs had a fear of being cornered, of being where he could not fight— worse still, being where he could not run if occasion demanded it. Out in the open, Saggs would have taken his chance, as he had done earlier in the evening.

"I'm about fed up on this," he told himself. "If it was me alone, I'd go out there and stage a wrestling match with that cop and try to make a get-away. But that wouldn't do now. Nope! It certainly and strictly would not. They might nab me and this bundle, find out where I worked—and then ask the boss to please explain."

Again he waited, while the perspiration streamed from him, fearing each moment that he would sneeze, and believing that a sneeze in that confined place would have the roar of a gun and draw the attention of every hated policeman within a quarter of a mile of the place.

Presently he believed that he could endure it no longer. Once more he crept down the ventilating shaft and so came to the little door, and this time he was more cautious, listening a moment before unfastening the catch and opening the door a couple of inches.

There was no light at all to be seen now, which pleased Saggs greatly. But he was in no undue hurry. He held his breath and listened, made certain that there was no lurking policeman standing in that dark hall.

Now he pressed the bundle under his left arm and close to his body. He opened the little door wider and crawled out into the hall. Crouched against the wall, he listened again for a time and then made his way swiftly to the room through which he had entered the house earlier in the evening.

He did not care to use the electric torch, and so had not taken it from the bundle. He wanted no flash of an electric lamp to betray him to the enemies of himself and The Thunderbolt. Into the little room he crept, and across it to the outside window, scarcely daring to breathe, listening intently all the time.

At the window he stopped and tried to peer out. The most of the lights along the driveway had been extinguished. The Camleigh home across the alley was illuminated, and Saggs grinned to think of what was going on there. He could imagine the ravings of a man who had been a victim of The Thunderbolt, and of detectives who could find no clew to lead them to the culprit. Knowing the motive for The Thunderbolt's work, Saggs relished the situation all the more.

He thought that he saw the flash of a light down by the alley wall, too, and it came to his mind that the police were still searching in the neighborhood, hoping to find something that would put them on the right trail.

Saggs confessed to himself that he was a little afraid, since his capture would mean so much to The Thunderbolt in addition to what it might mean for himself. He wished that he was half a dozen blocks away from the house. But there was only one way to get there, he told himself.

He opened the window wide and crawled out. In the pitch darkness near the wall of the house he watched and waited for a time, and then crept slowly and cautiously along the wall toward the side of the building.

Saggs had to cross the driveway and then the spacious lawn to reach the street. After that, he felt, he would be in the open, where a man always had a chance. He gathered his courage finally, and dashed across the driveway, making no more noise than a shadow.

Beside a clump of bushes he crouched, and finally went on as he had entered early in the evening, dodging from dark spot to dark spot, wondering for the first time in his life why the city wasted so much good money in providing street lights.

Now he was almost to the street. A couple of more silent dashes and he would be near the walk. He waited long enough to look around. The lights were still burning in front of the Brailson place, and a few automobiles were on the driveway, taking away the last guests to depart. Saggs could not see the Flatchley machine, and so he judged that John Flatchley already had driven away.

The street itself seemed to be empty as far as he could see. Everything looked all right, and Saggs began to have courage again. He made another dash, came to rest in the shadows once more. And for the second time that night his heart almost stood still because of a sudden and unexpected hail from near at hand.

"Put 'em up, you! No tryin' to dodge now!"

"A cop!" Saggs said to himself.

It came to him that this was the moment of greatest danger, that if he got through this all would be well. All he knew was that the man who had hailed him was to his left and a short distance behind him, probably beside the nearest tree.

Saggs sprang to his feet, bent double, and flew toward the street like a man with wings on his heels. Another hail came, he heard the roar of a weapon, and a bullet whistled past less than three feet from his head. This officer was not afraid to fire—no group of guests was in front of him.

There was nothing for Saggs to do except continue his headlong flight. To stop meant to be captured with that damning bundle beneath his arm. He did not think of throwing it from him. Even if he did that and was captured, he would have to explain his presence in the neighborhood, his lurking about the lawn, his sudden flight. And he would be traced, and John Flatchley asked to explain.

So he ran on, bending forward as much as possible. Another explosion came behind him, another bullet whistled past him, the officer shouted again—a warning and a threat.

Saggs heard the cry taken up behind him. He turned and dashed across the street before a limousine that had just left the Brailson house, causing the chauffeur to apply brakes and turn toward the nearest curb.

The pursuing policeman was disconcerted for an instant. He did not care to fire a shot into that limousine. Saggs did not realize this, but he did know that he had a moment's respite. He reached the walk on the other side of the street, ran on to another lawn, dodged into the shadows there, rushed on, his heart hammering at his ribs, his breath coming in little gasps.

He reached an alley, ran down it, got over a wall and into another yard. He did not know exactly where he was going, but he knew that he was putting distance between himself and danger, and that was what he desired mostly.

And suddenly he found that he was within a block and a half of the apartment house John Flatchley called home. He had evaded the pursuit, it seemed. Saggs ceased running, pressed the bundle closer against his side, got from the alley to the street, and walked down it like any belated pedestrian going home.

"Gosh!" Mr. Saggs gasped. "Gosh! This has been some night!"

CHAPTER IX

THE ADVENTURE'S END

DETECTIVE RADNER was keenly alive to the fact that this affair of The Thunderbolt would cause a cry from every part of the city that the police catch the culprit and cause him to suffer for his crimes. He knew also that the greatest cry would come from Wilson Camleigh, the latest victim of The Thunderbolt, a man who, because of his wealth, had considerable influence in political quarters.

In addition to these things, Detective Radner knew that his chief would have a few sarcastic remarks to make and a few orders to issue. It seemed ridiculous to Radner that no clew could be found by which The Thunderbolt could be traced.

"It's because he isn't a regular crook, living in the underworld and working with other crooks," Detective Radner told himself. "But if The Thunderbolt is John Flatchley, I'd like to know how he does it. Four stunts—and every one of them a whopper! From the way Camleigh howled, those stones must have been worth half a million."

Feeling that it was useless, Radner had the neighborhood searched well. Detectives were sent out from headquarters to aid him, but they discovered nothing of value. And neither Camleigh nor Cyrus Grantburg could give information that was worth anything.

Camleigh declared that he had seen The Thunderbolt's eyes, and that they were blue. Grantburg reminded Radner that this was his second experience with The Thunderbolt, and that he knew the rascal's eyes were black or dark brown. Camleigh said he was about five feet six inches tall, and Grantburg declared he was six feet or more. So Detective Martin Radner curled his lips in scorn and left the Camleigh residence.

The Brailson house was searched well before the guests began to depart and after they had gone. Radner sent some of the men back to headquarters, gave others certain orders, and then strolled through the house once more in search of John Flatchley.

Flatchley was not trying to avoid him, it was evident. Instead, John Flatchley sought him and engaged him in conversation.

"How much did he get from Camleigh?" Flatchley asked.

"A fortune in diamonds," said Radner.

"Seems to me that the police should catch the fellow."

"It isn't as easy as it sounds. And there is a reason," Detective Radner declared.

"You interest me."

"This fellow who calls himself The Thunderbolt is cute, all right, but the best of them make mistakes. I don't think he is a professional crook, and never did think so. He's after certain men, from the looks of things, and that fact may cause some of us to do a little hard thinking."

"Hard thinking stimulates the brain."

"And sometimes leads to results," Radner put in.

He told himself, as he turned away, that Flatchley puzzled him. Perhaps this scion of a well-known family was merely having a little fun with him, but Radner did not believe it.

"But how could he have done it?" the detective asked himself. "Unless my other guess is right— that Flatchley doesn't do it himself, but has some man who does at his orders. Maybe it's right, at that. I'll keep my eyes open."

He issued a few more orders, sent more men back to headquarters, and then began watching John Flatchley from afar. Flatchley, if he was aware of it, did not seem to care. He found Agnes Larimer and had a last dance with her. He called for his limousine, got into it with the ladies he was escorting, and drove away, chuckling as he told Brailson upon departing that he had had a splendid time.

The conversation in the limousine was of ordinary topics, since Miss Larimer's aunt was there. The Larimer residence reached, Flatchley escorted the ladies inside, but returned almost immediately.

"Boss, there's been a man keeping his eyes on this car," his chauffeur reported.

"What sort of a man?"

"I'd say he was a fly cop, only I don't see what a fly cop would want to watch this car for. He just went down the street."

"Your imagination is a corker," John Flatchley remarked. "Suppose we drive home now."

"Yes, sir."

The chauffeur started the car, and the limousine rolled slowly along the tree-bordered street. It turned into a narrow, dark side street, going toward the avenue and the apartment house. And suddenly the chauffeur gave a cry and put on the brakes, and the big car came to a stop.

Into the path of the headlights had stepped a man with a handkerchief over his face and a revolver in his hand, and the chauffeur remembered that there had been several holdups in the vicinity recently and that a certain belligerent chauffeur had been shot for making a show of resistance.

But this holdup man did not work alone, it appeared. Two others sprang from the darkness and wrenched open the doors. John Flatchley found himself covered with weapons. The chauffeur was forced to drive the car to the curb and stop again there.

"Keep 'em up!" a coarse voice growled into Flatchley's ear.

Flatchley made no reply. He put up his hands and leaned back against the cushions. But his eyes were busy. They inspected the two men who menaced him. Both were large men, both had handkerchiefs over their faces up to their eyes. Flatchley was especially interested in their hands and the weapons they held.

They searched him well, taking the few things of value to be found in his evening clothes. They went through his light overcoat, even inspecting the lining. Then they made him get out of the car, and while one guarded him well, the other searched the car's interior, examined the cushions, the carpet, the pockets.

The chauffeur was searched, too, and then John Flatchley was ordered back into the car and the chauffeur told to drive on. He needed no urging.

At a furious pace, he sent the limousine along the street and to the front entrance of the apartment house.

"I told you I saw somebody watchin' our car, sir," the chauffeur said.

"What did they get from you?" Flatchley wanted to know.

"About eight dollars, and a six-dollar watch."

"I'll fix that all right."

"But you are not to blame, sir. They probably got a lot from you."

"Not as much as they expected to get, I am

afraid," Flatchley replied. "Take the car to the garage. I'll report this affair."

He was chuckling as he walked through the lobby to the elevator. The colored elevator boy yawned and grinned as he started the car. John Flatchley returning in the early hours of the morning always meant a big tip.

But the elevator boy did not get his tip this time.

"Haven't a cent, George," he said. "I'm cleaned out."

"Them gamblin' houses is awful," the boy offered.

"Holdup, not gambling house."

"You been held up, boss?"

"In the limousine. Ask my chauffeur for all the details. If you wait until to-morrow, I think he'll have more details. He has a powerful imagination."

Flatchley chuckled again and hurried to his suite. He rang, but no Saggs opened the door for him. Flatchley used his night key, then snapped on the lights and made a quick survey of his suite. Then he hurried to the telephone and called police headquarters.

"This is Mr. John Flatchley," he said. "Is Detective Radner there?"

"I think he just came in," said the man at the desk. "Wait a moment, please."

A moment later Radner's deep voice came to him over the wire.

"I've been robbed, Radner—held up in my limousine," Flatchley reported. "They robbed my chauffeur, too. Three men—all large men wearing handkerchiefs as masks. Got some money, a ring, and a good watch from me, and a cheap watch and a few dollars from my chauffeur."

"Notice anything in particular about 'em?" Radner asked.

"Large men," Flatchley repeated. "Big feet and big hands. I got a good look at the two who handled me after they stopped the car. They both had me covered, Radner—and they both were handling *police special revolvers!* Get that? Police special revolvers, such as a man on the force must have. Some of your men been out trying to pick up a little easy money?"

"Where did the robbery take place?" Radner asked, after seeming to choke.

"It is too late in the night," observed Flatchley, "to ask or answer foolish questions. Where do you think it took place?"

Without another word he hung up the receiver on its hook and went into the living room.

"That should give Radner something to think about," John Flatchley told himself.

He tossed off hat and coat and sat down beside the long table and lighted a cigarette. He chuckled again and wondered what Detective Radner was thinking at that moment.

"So they wanted to search me unofficially, did

they?" Flatchley mused. "And they did it—and they didn't find the Camleigh loot, either. I'll make a bet with myself that everything taken from me and from the chauffeur will be returned to-morrow anonymously."

Then he began thinking of Saggs. Had everything gone right, Saggs should have been home some time before. Had Saggs met with disaster? Had he been unable to get out of the Brailson house? And what of The Thunderbolt's bundle— of the fortune in diamonds? Had Saggs found the stones, forgotten his loyalty to John Flatchley, turned ungrateful and dishonest?

"I'll bet he hasn't!" Flatchley told himself. "I'll bet on Saggs any day. But I wish he was here, and safe."

A slight noise came from the kitchen. John Flatchley dropped his cigarette and hurried quietly through the rooms. A moment he listened, and then he snapped on the lights.

He could see the cable of the dumbwaiter moving slowly, and knew that the box was coming up. He stepped back and watched. Now he could see the top of the box—and now it stopped. In the box was Saggs.

"Home, are you?" Flatchley said.

"Gosh, boss, but I've had an awful time! They even took a couple of shots at me. And I had to be careful they didn't follow me here."

"Did they?"

"They did not!" said Saggs.

"You have the bundle?"

"Sure thing, boss."

"Hand it here a moment."

Saggs handed it over. Flatchley spread it out, and from one of the pockets of the coat poured a stream of glittering gems. Saggs' eyes bulged.

"Gosh!"

"The loot," Flatchley explained.

"And once I almost threw that bundle away!" Saggs gasped.

CHAPTER X

HOUNDS AND PERFUME

NO, I'll not give up! I said that I'd catch this Thunderbolt, and I'm going to do it. He has been playing in luck, that's all. He is a common, ordinary man, and not some sort of god. And a common, ordinary man, no matter how clever he is, may make a serious mistake any day and be found out!"

So spoke Detective Martin Radner as he paced back and forth across the office of his chief, chewing on an unlighted cigar, his hat cocked on one side of his head, his eyes gleaming.

"It has been almost a month since The Thunderbolt made a move," the chief said.

"Yes. But he'll make a move—he'll make two more moves," Detective Radner declared.

"So you still think that The Thunderbolt is young John Flatchley?" asked his superior.

"I did think so once, and then I changed my mind," Radner admitted. "And now I'm on the fence. I do not know whether The Thunderbolt is John Flatchley, but if he is I'll know it soon."

"He's a smooth customer, whoever he is," said the chief. "And if he pulls off another stunt, and we don't catch him, we'll never hear the last of it. He has robbed four of the richest men in town——"

"He has robbed four of the sacred Big Six," Radner interrupted. "And if I am not mistaken he'll rob the other two; attempt it, at any rate."

There was silence for a few seconds, save for the sound of Radner's heavy feet as he paced the floor of the private office, from corner to corner, like a wild beast in a cage. Both Radner and his chief were thinking what The Thunderbolt had done.

"What have you arranged now?" the chief asked hopefully, breaking the silence.

"Dogs!"

"Beg pardon?"

"Bloodhounds!" said Radner. "I've arranged with the sheriff's office. They have some of the best dogs in the country over there. And when I call for them——"

"Mean to say you're going after The Thunderbolt with hounds the same as you'd go after a murderer out in the country?"

"Yes, sir."

"How can you trail a man over city pavements? Suppose he uses a motor car."

"If he uses a motor car the trail is liable to end where he gets into the car," Detective Radner said. "It is only a chance, of course. But the main thing now is to discover whether John Flatchley is The Thunderbolt."

"How are you going to do that?" the chief wanted to know.

Detective Martin Radner took from his pocket something that caused the chief to sit forward in his chair. It was an atomizer, a tiny one, the bulb of which easily could be concealed in the palm of the hand.

"See that?" the detective asked. "Baby atomizer. It is filled with a scent that I had a great deal of trouble securing. This scent is terribly strong when a man gets the first whiff of it—and then his nose refuses to smell it again."

"How's that?" the chief asked.

"His sense of smell is what you might call paralyzed by it. After the first few whiffs his sense of smell is neutral as far as this scent is concerned. I can't explain it, but——"

"I understand what you mean," the chief interrupted. "He gets so used to it that he doesn't notice it at all?"

"Exactly."

"And what are you going to do with the stuff, Radner?" the chief asked.

"I'm going to spray it on John Flatchley," Detective Radner replied, "on his shoes and the bottom of his trousers."

"Radner, don't be an ass! If Flatchley is The Thunderbolt he'd probably change clothes before going to work."

"Possibly. But this scent will cling to him, chief. If Flatchley is The Thunderbolt, and he makes a move within three or four days after I have put this scent on him, the dogs can pick up the trail at the scene of the crime. I can get the scent on him to-night."

"Where and how?"

"The Garslens have a silver wedding anniversary, and all society will be present. Flatchley is going. The affair lasts only from six until nine, because of Mrs. Garslen's ill health. The guests will leave early—understand? I'm on guard to-night. There will be a fortune in gifts."

"Oh, yes, I remember now."

"I'll get the scent on him and then trust to luck. Of course, he may not be The Thunderbolt. Or, if he is, he may leave the scene of his next crime and get into a motor car. Or he may not make a move for several days, by which time the scent will be lost. It is only a chance, but I am trying everything to catch The Thunderbolt. He may have quit work in town and gone elsewhere. But I haven't given up!"

"And I'm glad of it," the chief replied. "I say again that I think it is all nonsense to suspect John Flatchley. He'd have too much at stake."

"But he's just the sort of man to do it," said Radner. "He is courageous, witty, loves adventure, and would think that he was acting from a good motive. But a thief is a thief, of course, whatever his motive."

"Well, whoever The Thunderbolt is, I hope that you get your hands on him and keep them there," the chief declared. "If he robs another of The Big Six, and we do not land him, we're going to hear an awful howl from these precious financiers of ours. I'm sick of all this talk about the incompetency of the police force. Go to it, Radner, and may good luck be with you!"

Detective Radner ceased pacing the floor, threw away the cigar he had been chewing, took a fresh one from his waistcoat pocket, and lighted it.

"Bloodhounds and perfume!" the chief said with a grunt. "It is a new combination, but maybe it will work. I hope so, at least. And don't forget, Radner, that there's a big reward."

"To blazes with the big reward!" Detective Martin Radner exclaimed. "The Thunderbolt made a fool of me on two occasions, and I am not forgetting the bars of a cell, whoever he is!"

"I'll have a nice, sunny cell with southern exposure cleaned out and properly aired, and redecorated, too, if you say the word," said the chief, chuckling.

Detective Radner's face flushed.

"There seems to be an idea around headquarters that The Thunderbolt is too much for me," he said. "Maybe he is, and maybe again he isn't. We'll see!"

"If he is too much for you, then he is a particularly smooth article," the chief declared, eager to pour oil on the troubled waters. "Don't let any little jest throw you off the track, Radner. You get The Thunderbolt!"

Without making reply Detective Martin Radner hurried from the chief's private office. He puffed furiously at his cigar, thus revealing his state of mind. The gleam of determination was still in his eyes.

CHAPTER XI

THE ATOMIZER

LATE that evening, standing behind a bank of ferns and bloom, Detective Martin Radner, feeling awkward in his evening clothes, saw John Flatchley, resplendent in his, coming slowly up the broad staircase.

The silver wedding reception had attracted a large number of guests because of the popularity of the host and hostess. Detective Radner and two assistants were there to keep their eyes on the valuable anniversary gifts, but in reality Radner allowed the other two men to do that, while he kept an eye on John Flatchley.

Flatchley had arrived at an early hour, escorting Agnes Larimer. The closest observer could not have seen anything peculiar or extraordinary in John Flatchley's conduct. Certainly he neither looked nor acted like a criminal.

He was immensely popular and had chatted and laughed with his friends and acquaintances, paid polite compliments to his hostess and host, and seemed to be having a pleasant evening. And now, without doubt, he was ascending to the second floor to visit the smoking room and smoke a cigarette.

Detective Martin Radner observed him well as he passed. Flatchley was humming a song, and there was a smile upon his lips. But Radner had been a detective with a reputation for too long a time to judge a man entirely by the cast of his countenance.

John Flatchley went along the hall and turned into the smoking room, and Detective Radner followed, attempting to act as though he had just happened to loiter along that way. When he entered, John Flatchley was in the act of lighting a cigarette. For the moment there was nobody else in the room.

"Well, if it isn't my old friend, Detective Radner!" Flatchley exclaimed. "I fancied that I saw you on the lower floor about half an hour ago."

"I'm on the job," Radner admitted.

"Ah! Keeping an eye on the presents?"

"Yes."

"But the presents are in a room on the lower floor, I believe," Flatchley said, smiling.

"Oh, I've got two good men down there," Radner rejoined.

"Good enough! And you are watching the rest of the house, what? Keeping an eye on me now? Think that I am liable to stuff my pockets with my host's cigars?"

"I guess you can buy your own," the detective said. "Some crowd to-night, eh?"

"A splendid occasion," Flatchley replied. "When a man and a woman can exist together in matrimony for a quarter of a century, they are entitled to give a party."

Flatchley puffed lazily at his cigarette and walked toward the nearest easy-chair. Detective Radner followed him closely. Flatchley wondered a bit at the detective's manner. Why did the detective seek to enter a conversation when he should know that he would come out second best, in case of repartee, when he easily could watch Flatchley from a distance? Flatchley had noticed that Radner had attempted to get close to him several times during the evening. He had overheard Radner talking to one of his assistants, too—and what had been said had both amused and surprised him.

Radner sat down in another chair and touched match to cigar. John Flatchley watched him narrowly through a blue cloud of fragrant smoke.

"Haven't caught The Thunderbolt yet, have you?" Flatchley asked suddenly.

Detective Radner removed his cigar from between his lips and looked the other man straight in the eyes.

"We haven't caught him yet," Radner admitted. "There are some things that may be accomplished in a hurry—and others may take considerable time."

"Oh, I see! This is one of the things that takes considerable time, eh?"

"Yes. The Thunderbolt is no fool," Detective Radner said. "If he was within the hearing of my voice now I'd tell him that he has shown extreme cleverness. Give credit where credit is due. He is clever—so the more credit to the man who catches him."

"And you expect to be that man, eh? Still trying? Still going after him?"

"Oh, yes, still trying," Radner replied. "But The Thunderbolt hasn't made a move for some time."

"Possibly he has gone from our fair city," Flatchley said, "to spend his ill-gotten gains elsewhere."

"Possibly, but I do not think so," Detective Radner replied, puffing at his cigar and glancing at Flatchley again. "I expect to have him rob two more men, unless he is caught robbing the first of them."

As he spoke Detective Radner watched John Flatchley closely, but if his words had any significance for Flatchley, or disturbed him in the least, he certainly did not show it. As a matter of fact he stifled a yawn.

"Two more victims, eh?" Flatchley said. "Hope that I am not one of them! But I'm a poor man compared to the fellows The Thunderbolt has been robbing. He picks out the big financiers, so I suppose I need not be alarmed."

"He has made fools of the police department,"

Detective Radner declared. "But we'll get him if he continues his work, if he remains in town."

"Confident, aren't you?"

"Yes, sir!" said Radner. "We made a mistake in underestimating The Thunderbolt at first. We thought he was an ordinary, professional criminal. But we are ready for him now. We admit that he is a clever man, but we are not afraid of his making laughingstocks of us any more. If he makes another move we'll get him! But he may not make another move; he may be afraid!"

Once more Detective Radner watched Flatchley closely, and John Flatchley did nothing but smile.

"If The Thunderbolt heard you say that he might look upon it as a sort of dare," Flatchley said. "And, from what I have heard of The Thunderbolt, he doesn't seem to be the sort to grow afraid easily."

"Maybe he's lost his nerve," Detective Radner said.

"What makes you think so?"

"He hasn't made a move for a month. If he hasn't lost his nerve he'll be making a move soon. If he doesn't within the week I'll commence to think that The Thunderbolt, whoever he is, either has left town, or else is afraid to turn another trick."

Detective Radner glanced quickly at John Flatchley as he spoke, but there was no expression on Flatchley's face to indicate that he was taking this accusation of cowardice to himself. For the thousandth time Detective Martin Radner told himself that Flatchley was not The Thunderbolt, and in the next instant told himself, for the thousandth time, that he was! This affair of The Thunderbolt was getting on Radner's nerves, which had the effect of making him all the more determined and relentless.

Flatchley, having finished his cigarette, got slowly out of the chair, and Radner did the same. John Flatchley yawned and glanced at a wall clock in one corner of the room.

"Well, this affair is about at an end," he observed. "Better find the lady I am escorting and prepare to leave, I suppose. What you have said about The Thunderbolt interests me, Radner. Detective work must have its fascinating moments."

"But not all its moments are fascinating," Radner admitted. "It isn't all glory and romance, you know."

"I suppose not. Yet there is something fascinating in a man hunt," Flatchley replied. "The joy in the man hunt is a natural trait of the human being. Because we can't go out and hunt men all the time we go after ducks and rabbits and deer. Human beings are peculiar things; they enjoy the hunt, yet the sympathy nine times out of ten is with the hunted. How do you explain that?"

"I don't attempt to explain it," Detective Radner answered. "But there is a lot of misplaced sympathy in the world.   A crook, for instance, is nothing but a crook."

"Oh, I suppose so," said John Flatchley, stifling another yawn.

He walked slowly across the room toward the hall door and stopped for a moment to admire some particular, fine-cut flowers that had been placed on a pedestal near the doorway. Detective Martin Radner was at his heels.

Radner had a handkerchief in his hand, and now he dropped it and stooped quickly to pick it up. As he did so his right hand, carrying the little atomizer, was within a few inches of John Flatchley's feet. Radner did his work quickly and then stood up, returning the handkerchief to one pocket and the atomizer to another.

"Radner, that's an atrocious perfume you use," John Flatchley said suddenly. "I got a whiff of it as you bent over.   Heavens, man!"

"Made a mistake and got too much on," Radner said, as though a bit embarrassed. "I don't do this fancy-clothes stuff very often, and I'm not up on the fine points."

"Here is one," said Flatchley. "Throw your perfume away, or give it to some one who is more accustomed to using such cheap stuff."

"That's good perfume," Radner declared.

"You can buy good dill pickles, too," observed

Mr. Flatchley, "but you wouldn't go to a social affair carrying a couple in your hands, would you?"

John Flatchley went into the hall and descended the broad staircase again. Detective Martin Radner, stopping behind the bank of ferns and bloom, grinned and chuckled softly to himself.

"Never suspected," Radner told himself. "Thought I had the stuff on me. And by now he isn't able to smell it himself. If he is The Thunderbolt and pulls a trick within a couple of days, I've got him!"

On the floor below Flatchley found himself in a jam of men and women preparing to leave, in the midst of a thousand perfumes, where that which he carried mingled with the others and could not be distinguished from the rest.

He found Miss Larimer, and a few minutes later they had left the house and were in Flatchley's limousine and rolling through the streets toward Miss Agnes Larimer's home.

"John!" she gasped, holding a handkerchief to her nostrils suddenly.

"What is it, my dear girl?" Flatchley asked.

"I'd not have thought it of you, John. And perhaps it would be the polite thing to ignore it. But if I am going to marry you one of these days I must take an interest in you and see that you do things properly."

"I suppose so. What crime have I committed now?"

"I believe, from what my nostrils tell me, that you have bathed in cheap perfume."

Flatchley chuckled. "You won't be able to smell it in a couple of minutes," he said.

"I should think not. By that time my sense of smell will be utterly paralyzed," Agnes said. "But what on earth——"

"That is good perfume," Flatchley declared. "I did not put it on myself. Somebody else put it on— a detective. Radner was at the house, you know, supposedly guarding the presents. In reality he was watching me."

"John! Then he still suspects?"

"Yes, and no," said Flatchley. "He does, and he doesn't. Radner is no fool. One moment he is satisfied that I am The Thunderbolt, and the next he is sure that I am not. But he is—er—determined to find out for certain."

"Then there is danger, John!"

"Nonsense!" Flatchley exclaimed. "There is no such thing as danger, nothing more than a continual battle of wits. Do not be afraid for me, Agnes."

"I know what you are doing, John dear, and I appreciate the motive behind your acts. I want you to finish your work. But I'll be very glad when it is all over."

"I believe I will also," Flatchley replied. "Two more little enterprises, and then we make an end of The Thunderbolt."

"Do you have to do two more, John?"

"It wouldn't be fair to rob four and not the other two of The Big Six."

"But isn't it more dangerous now than it was before?"

"I wouldn't say it was more dangerous. But it does call forth a bit more skill and watchfulness."

"And that perfume——"

"Oh, Detective Radner had it," Flatchley replied easily. "Say no more about it, dear girl! And do not worry, please."

"And when are you going to be through, John?"

"Very soon, my dear. Two more little enterprises, as I said. I have been quiet for a month or so, just to get them guessing. Now I am going to strike two blows in quick succession—and that'll be the end of it."

"And when——"

"My dear girl, do not ask me straight questions, please," John Flatchley said. "As I have told you before I do not want you to know anything. So, if disaster comes, you'll not be involved. But disaster will not come. I flatter myself that my plans are perfect."

"You must be careful, John. I am so afraid for you at times. The law never would take your motives into consideration, of course. And if you were caught, John, you'd be disgraced, lose your position in society, and possibly have to go to prison. And what would become of me?"

"Rather pessimistic, aren't you?" Flatchley said, chuckling. "Do not worry, Agnes—please. Two more little enterprises, and then—then The Thunderbolt ceases to exist—and John Flatchley goes on his honeymoon."

He drew her toward him and kissed her. The limousine pulled up before the door of her home.

CHAPTER XII

PREPARING A JOKE

SAGGS stood before the mirror and studied his reflection. He was almost moved to laughter at it. Mr. Saggs was not a Greek god, and he knew it, and, as has been said before, he gloried in his ugliness. Now and then he surveyed his reflection in a mirror and wondered how it happened that John Flatchley kept him around.

It was almost ten o'clock now, and Saggs expected Flatchley at any moment. He knew that the reception was over at nine, and Flatchley had dropped the hint that he would return to his rooms as soon as possible after escorting his fiancée to her home.

Saggs wondered whether this was to be the night for work as The Thunderbolt. As a matter of fact Saggs liked a bit of excitement occasionally though each of The Thunderbolt's adventures caused him some hours of extreme anxiety.

Turning away from the mirror and the contemplation of his image in it, Saggs went quickly around the big living room to make sure that everything was as it should be. He drew down a shade over a court window, snapped on another electric light, and knew that the pleasant room was ready for John Flatchley's return.

No sooner was this done than the buzzer sounded, and Saggs hurried through the little hall to the corridor door, unfastened the catch, and pulled the door open. Flatchley entered and walked through to the living room. Saggs followed to take his hat, coat, and gloves.

The wine of anticipation was running riot in the veins of Saggs now, but no inkling of the fact showed in his face. His countenance was that inscrutable mask so often worn by good servants. He disposed of hat, coat, and gloves in the regulation manner and then returned to the living room and approached John Flatchley, who had seated himself in an easy-chair beside the table and was lighting a cigarette.

"Anything else, sir?" Saggs asked.

"A glass of ice water," Flatchley ordered.

Saggs' eyelids flickered a bit as he started to get it. When John Flatchley drank ice water it meant that his brain was at work, and that adventure impended. Saggs returned quickly with the drink and stood by while Flatchley drank it.

"Saggs!"

"Sir?" Saggs said.

"You are sniffing! Who are you sniffing, Saggs?"

"I—er—there was an odor——" Saggs muttered.

"Explain yourself, Saggs."

"Some sort of a perfume, sir. I got a strong whiff of it a moment ago, but now it seems to have passed away, sir. Possibly the chauffeur has been using some sort of disinfectant in the limousine, sir."

"I certainly hope he has not used one so powerful. That was perfume you smelled, Saggs, and not disinfectant. It is on me."

"Sir?" Saggs gasped in horror.

That John Flatchley could use perfume at all was bad enough, to Saggs' way of thinking, but that he could use one like this was beyond belief.

"Yes, I've taken to using a distinctive perfume, Saggs," John Flatchley said.

"It—it certainly is distinctive, sir, if you'll pardon me," Saggs replied with a trace of sarcasm.

"Do you mean to tell me, Saggs, that you do not approve of it?" Flatchley asked.

"Er—perhaps it is something new, sir—the latest —some new fad. However, it is not lasting. I cannot smell it now."

"I suppose not," Flatchley said. "It is so strong that it puts a person's sense of smell out of commission. It is quite powerful—quite!"

"Quite!" Saggs agreed.

There was a merry twinkle in Flatchley's eyes that Saggs could not help seeing, and he took heart. Flatchley was up to some joke, he supposed, else the powerful perfume was a part of some plan Flatchley was making.

"Saggs, I no longer am John Flatchley. I now am The Thunderbolt!"

Saggs gasped, grinned, and then stepped closer to the table. That change meant that he was a comrade-in-arms now, and not a servant.

"Gosh, boss," he said. "I thought you never was goin' to again."

"Don't start in talking like a tough, now."

"But it's been more'n a month, boss. Gosh! I'd begun to think we never was goin' to have some more fun."

"Fun, you call it?"

"Well—adventure, then. I sure am glad, boss. So you're goin' after another of The Big Six, are you?"

"I am," The Thunderbolt declared. "The next on the list is Mr. Francis Malberton. Know anything about him, Saggs?"

"Only that he's one of them Big Six guys."

"He's an old bachelor," The Thunderbolt explained. "Been too stingy all his life to support a wife. But he's got a big, old-fashioned house and a couple of mediocre servants. Got the house on a mortgage, I suppose."

"Skinflint, is he?" Saggs asked.

"An appropriate term," The Thunderbolt admitted. "Skinflint he is. I never did know exactly what the word means, but it sounds like it meant enough. Francis Malberton is a skinflint and a swindler."

"All them guys are," Saggs agreed.

"I have been spending a great deal of the past month investigating, in a careful and private manner, the affairs of Francis Malberton," The Thunderbolt admitted. "It appears at this juncture that the said Francis Malberton is in a hole."

"Broke?" Saggs asked.

"Dear me, no!" The Thunderbolt replied. "He has, however, turned most of his money into negotiable bonds and unset diamonds. Francis Malberton, if you gather my meaning, has been skating on thin ice. The ice is about to break with him. So he—er—is throwing off extra weight."

"Aw, boss, talk sense!" Saggs begged.

"Very well. Malberton has been caught in a jam, and the only way out is to make restitution. But he has been getting himself into a position where he can go through court proceedings and emerge with most of his coin. He has a box of easily negotiable bonds which he intends to put in some safe place. He has arranged matters so that he can show he has lost his fortune through injudicious investments. Cleared of the debts by the court, he then will dig up his bonds and enjoy life again, and no man can hinder him."

"I think I getcha, boss."

"Thank you."

"And you're goin' to get that box of bonds?"

"I am," said The Thunderbolt. "But, if I took those bonds and converted them to my own use I would be aiding him, in a way, in swindling some innocent persons. But I have an excellent plan, Saggs. When we get through with Francis Malberton he will be as broke as he wishes to pretend."

"But if you don't take that box——"

"I intend taking the box, Saggs—and another box also."

"Another?" Saggs gasped.

"Precisely. Francis Malberton has two boxes. One is filled with bonds, and he will have to hide that for some time in order to carry out his plan. The other is also filled with articles of value, and Mr. Malberton has an idea, I take it, that nobody suspects it is in existence. But enough of that. It need not interest you now. I do not care to confound you with too many details. I have my plan all worked out."

"I'll bet you have!" said Saggs. "To-night?"

"To-night, Saggs. You have guessed it. Now there are other things. At the social affair where I was a guest this evening Detective Martin Radner was present."

"Boss! You want to watch out for that guy!"

"Afraid of Mart Radner, Saggs? I am a bit surprised."

"Aw, I ain't afraid for myself—ain't afraid of

any cop in the world," Saggs declared. "But that Radnor man is bad medicine. He's no fool."

"He'd be greatly complimented if he heard you say that, Saggs. He is no fool. But neither are we fools."

"You may not be," Saggs said. "I ain't so sure about myself sometimes."

"I saw Detective Radner," The Thunderbolt went on. "I overheard him speaking to another detective who was watching the presents. Some detectives are a rum lot, Saggs."

"They sure are, boss."

"Yes. For instance a detective may be watching a man, but he seldom takes the trouble to realize that the man may be watching him at the same time. I watched Radner. I overheard his interesting conversation with the other detective."

"About you?" Saggs asked.

"About dogs," The Thunderbolt corrected.

"Dogs?"

"Bloodhounds!" said The Thunderbolt.

"Gosh!" Saggs' eyes bulged for an instant.

"He is going to use hounds," The Thunderbolt explained. "When The Thunderbolt turns his next trick an effort will be made to trail him with the dogs. Suppose, Saggs, that the dogs picked up my scent to-night and followed me—here."

"Then Radner would know——"

"Precisely!" said The Thunderbolt. "The trail

could be broken, of course, by getting into a motor car."

"Sure, boss!" Saggs said. "You could do that all right."

"But I do not intend using a motor car," The Thunderbolt replied. "I do intend, however, to have some fun with Detective Radner. The perfume that displeased you is a part of it, Saggs."

"I thought you must be usin' it for some special purpose," Saggs observed. "It's some perfume, if you ask me."

"I'll admit that it is. Saggs, I went to the smoking room in the house where I was to-night, and Detective Radner followed me and engaged me in conversation."

"Slung some talk, did you?"

"We did. I gathered from his speech that he still has a faint suspicion that I am The Thunderbolt."

"Then we'll have to be careful, boss," Saggs said quickly.

"We are always careful," The Thunderbolt said. "He mentioned that The Thunderbolt had not been working lately, and he threw me, now and then, an insinuation, but I trust that I did not betray myself by the expression of my face."

"I'll bet you didn't, boss!"

"Then we started to leave the room, Saggs. Detective Radner, clumsy fellow, dropped his handkerchief. He stooped to pick it up while I was admiring some flowers. As he did so he squirted this perfume over my shoes and the bottoms of my trousers, using a small atomizer."

"Boss!" Saggs gasped.

"Detective Radner, being eager and excited, failed to notice that there was a mirror on the wall in front of me. I observed his rather peculiar action; and afterward I smelled the perfume, of course, and allowed him to think that I thought it was on him."

"Then——" Saggs began, but The Thunderbolt raised a hand commanding silence.

"It is a rather peculiar perfume," The Thunderbolt continued, "but it happens that I am acquainted with it. I even have a small phial of it in the other room. It is used for many purposes; sometimes to dispel the odor left by a disinfectant. It clings, Saggs—clings! And the stuff is on my shoes and the bottoms of these trousers. It has penetrated by this time to undergarments and to the skin itself."

"Gosh!" said Saggs.

"Detective Radner's idea, of course, is that if I am The Thunderbolt and turn a trick before a couple of days are over, I'll leave a trail the dogs can follow easily. He'll give the dogs a whiff of the perfume—a little whiff so their sense of smell will not be ruined for a time—and then they will nose the trail and run The Thunderbolt down. It is quite an idea!"

"Boss!" Saggs gasped. "You'll have to be careful. You ought to wait a few days before——"

"But I intend to do some work to-night," The Thunderbolt declared. "And I cannot allow Detective Radner to interfere with my plans. As soon as we have finished this little talk, Saggs, you will prepare a hot bath for me, returning to your status as valet a few minutes for that purpose."

"I getcha! That wipes out the odor."

"I'll bathe carefully and put on fresh clothing. I'll even put on something that will kill the slightest odor that might be remaining. And then I'll go out and attend to the case of Mr. Francis Malberton."

"I getcha, boss! When they don't find that perfume trail they'll think you ain't The Thunderbolt."

"Not so fast, Saggs. They are going to find a trail. But where it will lead them—— Oh, Saggs, where it will lead them!"

"I don't quite getcha now, boss."

"You, Saggs, are to help to-night."

"I'm glad of that."

"We'll both visit the residence of Mr. Malberton. And you will have these shoes of mine with you."

"With that perfume on 'em?"

"Exactly," said The Thunderbolt. "And the dogs will trail you."

Saggs gulped and licked at his lips.

"Boss, I can't outrun no dogs," he explained. "And if they tracked me here——"

"But nobody is going to track you here, Saggs," The Thunderbolt interrupted. "I am preparing a bit of fun, you see; a jest. You get the bath ready, and when I have bathed and dressed I'll tell you the remainder of the plan. If everything goes smoothly Detective Martin Radner is going to be one puzzled man to-night. He may even suspect that I had something to do with the affair—but I'd like to see him prove it."

CHAPTER XIII

THE BUTTON

THE hour of midnight struck. The Thunderbolt slipped quietly into the kitchen, followed by Saggs. No lights were turned on. The door of the dumb-waiter chute was opened, and The Thunderbolt listened for a time. And then he drew the dumb-waiter up. It made not the slightest noise. The dumb-waiter was kept in perfect condition under Saggs' supervision.

"I'll have to go first to-night," The Thunderbolt said. "Careful, now!"

"Yes, sir!"

"It's been a month since we've done anything like this, Saggs, but we don't want to be rusty to-night. A little miscalculation and it will be all over."

"There won't be any of that miscalculation stuff, boss," Saggs declared.

The Thunderbolt got into the dumb-waiter and was lowered rapidly to the basement. There he got out and stood back in the darkness and listened for a moment, and then he sent the dumb-waiter up again, and Saggs, carrying a small package, came down in turn. They stood some distance apart in

142

the darkness of the basement, stretching their cramped muscles, and then The Thunderbolt gave a slight hiss to attract Saggs' attention and led the way to the hall and through it, past the door of the room where the superintendent slept, and to a little door that opened on the alley used by tradesmen.

With a key he took from one of his pockets The Thunderbolt unlocked this door, opened it, peered forth, and listened. He slipped out with Saggs after him; the door was locked behind them, and they separated. The Thunderbolt went through the dark alley to the nearest street; Saggs went quietly through the same alley in the opposite direction.

When he reached the street The Thunderbolt made sure that nobody was in sight, especially persons who might know him. He crossed the street and walked along it rapidly, always alert. He came to a cross street where the walks were shaded by big trees, and turned into it. The residence of Francis Malberton was but a few blocks away from the fashionable apartment house where John Flatchley had his rooms.

Without meeting any one The Thunderbolt came to the corner of the Malberton property and quickly slipped over an old-fashioned iron picket fence and got inside. He crouched in the shadow of a clump of brush for a moment and then crept on toward the house. Near a basement window he came to a stop.

It was so dark there that he could see nothing, and

he did not care to flash his electric torch. He stood against the wall and waited. Five minutes he waited, and then a faint hiss came to him through the darkness. The Thunderbolt answered it in kind, and Saggs slipped through the darkness and to his side.

"You came by the alley?" The Thunderbolt whispered.

"Just as you told me, boss. There's no guard here at all, unless he is inside."

"You remember what I told you?"

"Every word, boss."

"If you make a mistake, Saggs——"

"I won't make any mistake, boss. I've got the whole thing down pat! We're goin' to have the laugh on that Radner man."

"That's the spirit, Saggs! All ready now?"

"Yes, sir."

The Thunderbolt turned away from him and toward the basement window. He drew rubber gloves over his hands and put on the long black hood with its peculiar device on the front of it. His eyes gleamed through two tiny slits. From a pocket he took an instrument, and a few seconds later the basement window had been opened.

Swiftly The Thunderbolt slipped inside the house and flashed his electric torch. He knew well the arrangement of the interior of this house by reason of his visits as a guest in the old days, when it had not belonged to Francis Malberton, but to an old family of the city.

Through the basement he went, and up a flight of stairs to the first floor of the residence. There he stopped in the hall for a few seconds to listen. He knew where the two old servants slept on the second floor, and he was not worried about them.

Along the hall he crept toward the front of the big house, and after a time he reached a spot where he could see a faint gleam of light coming from beneath the door of the library. The Thunderbolt put his electric torch back into his pocket, took out an automatic pistol, and crept toward the door.

Francis Malberton, a tall, slender, hawk-nosed man of about fifty-five, sat in his library that night after the hour of twelve, with a mass of papers and documents on the table before him.

The library was an old-fashioned room, the furnishings were shabby, and there were quantities of dust everywhere. The two servants whom Malberton kept for little more than their board, an old man and his wife, could not be expected to clean the big house more than every few days.

Malberton worked beneath a single incandescent light that hung over the table, and the corners of the big room were in darkness. Twice as many articles of furniture were in the room as there should have been, and they cast deep shadows.

But Francis Malberton saw nothing except the

piles of papers in front of him. He was planning the last and greatest swindle of his career, and he wanted to be certain that he had every detail correct. An oversight might cause disaster.

Malberton was one of those financiers who now and then are caught by the same bait they cast. Though the other members of The Big Six did not know it, and did not even suspect it, Malberton had been dabbling in financial affairs in other quarters, and he had been swindled even as he had swindled others.

But he made no outcry about it. He smiled grimly and then deliberately planned another swindle of his own, and managed to get back his losses with more than the ordinary interest. But this time he went a shade over the line in his eagerness, and he found himself in difficulties. Then he made his big plan.

An expert examining the papers would say that Francis Malberton was on the verge of bankruptcy. Malberton expected to have that said of him within a few days. He had the fortune in bonds, and that he would put in a safe place. He had another fortune, and that would be concealed, also.

He was safe from a criminal charge, his attorney had assured him, but not from civil suits to recover money. These civil suits, the same attorney had declared, would go against him, and he would be stripped of funds. But as matters stood now, the suits would come, Malberton would go through a bankruptcy court, and, when things were settled, he still would have a fortune to enjoy. A little thing like concealing assets did not bother Francis Malberton, so long as he was not caught at it.

Of course, if the bonds were located, and that other mysterious box was unearthed also, then Francis Malberton would find himself stripped of his wealth, as he had stripped so many others, but he did not expect to have such a thing happen.

The box of bonds bothered him a bit. He was not afraid of the second box, because the assets in it had been gathered through the years, and he did not believe it known that he possessed them. But he feared at times that the bonds might be unearthed. Some shrewd lawyer might discover the purchases he had made and force him to disclose what had become of the bonds. Even then Malberton would emerge from the mess with that second fortune, of which men knew nothing.

But Malberton had his papers almost in order, papers that he had made out himself, and which showed how his fortune had dwindled, supposedly, through bad investments, so that very little of it remained. His creditors, of course, would take this old house, and some other parcels of real estate he owned, but which did not amount to much. Malberton could take things easily and carefully until discharged by the bankruptcy court, and then he could laugh and enjoy the wealth for the remainder of his days.

Now he bent over the table, squinted through his eyeglasses, and added a long row of figures in an effort to make the total the same as one in the ledger at his elbow. He had discovered that it is no easy task to doctor books.

No sound reached his ears save the scratching of the pencil with which he worked, and the rustling of the trees at the side of the house as the night wind shook their branches. But a peculiar feeling seemed to come over him suddenly.

He raised his head and listened intently, but could hear no unusual sound. Once more he bent over the sheets of paper before him, picked up a sharp pencil, and attacked the long columns of figures. Yet he could not shake off the peculiar feeling. Something seemed to be warning him of danger.

Again he raised his head, the pencil poised in the air. He shivered, though he could not tell why. There was a carafe near at hand; he poured out a glass of water and tossed it off. His nervousness had increased, and he tried to tell himself that there was no sense in it. It was as though his dead conscience had come to life. The thought made him grin.

Now he was possessed by the feeling that he was being watched, that there was danger behind him. He tried to force himself to turn his head, but at first he could not. His will power, upon which he so long had prided himself, seemed to have weakened for the time being.

Finally he made an effort and turned his head slowly, fearfully, telling himself that nothing could be there to alarm him, yet at the same time realizing that there must be, to cause him to feel so.

From one corner of the big room, where the shadows were deepest, a shadow seemed to float toward him. Francis Malberton gave a little gasp and sank down into his chair.

The shadow moved closer, and then Malberton would have cried out, except that the sound seemed to choke in his throat, and he could no more than give a low gurgle that wasn't heard a dozen feet away.

He saw that a man had come from the shadows in the corner of the room and now stood before him, and at the first glance he knew that the man was The Thunderbolt.

There was the devilish black hood with the design on the front of it. There stood The Thunderbolt, dressed all in black, his hands covered with black rubber gloves, and one of those hands was holding an automatic pistol that menaced Francis Malberton in an efficient fashion.

"Not a sound out of you—not a sound!" The Thunderbolt warned, speaking in a low tone that carried to Malberton's ears, but not outside the room.

Fear-stricken, Francis Malberton could not have made a sound at the moment had he dared to do so. He was the most cowardly of all The Big Six when it came to physical things. His vocal chords seemed suddenly paralyzed, and the perspiration broke out on his forehead, his face, his hands.

The Thunderbolt's eyes glittered through the slits in the hood he wore. He took a step nearer Francis Malberton, and the financier settled down farther in his chair.

"So!" The Thunderbolt said. "We meet at last, Mr. Malberton. To-night it is your turn to contribute funds to me. And you are going to contribute handsomely, too."

"No—no!" Malberton gasped thickly. "I am not a rich man. I am ruined now. See these papers! I have been figuring—figuring! My investments have all gone wrong. My fortune has been swept away. I must go into bankruptcy——"

"I did not come here to be entertained, Mr. Malberton," The Thunderbolt interrupted.

'But I am telling you the truth! Look at these books—read the story they tell!"

"I am by no means an expert accountant, and I judge that it would take a genuine expert to make head or tail of those books of yours," The Thunderbolt replied, chuckling behind his hood. "Suppose we cease this comedy."

"But——"

"Have you an idea that I know nothing, that I do not take the trouble to gather information?" The Thunderbolt interrupted again. "Poverty-stricken, are you? I think not! I probably know almost as much about your business as you do yourself. Now, Mr. Malberton, we'll get along a lot better if you just obey orders and do not attempt anything foolish, either in word or action."

"But—but I tell you——" Malberton began.

"And I'm telling you that you'll get a couple of bullets through your body if you don't cease this meaningless mouthing and get down to business!"

"Wh-what do you want?" Malberton gasped.

"That is much better. I want a certain box, Mr. Malberton—a box that contains a sum in negotiable bonds."

"You—you—— What box can you mean?" Malberton cried. "I have no box of bonds. I am on the verge of bankruptcy, I tell you!"

"Still inclined to play the comedian, are you?" The Thunderbolt asked. "I had hoped, sir, that I'd be able to carry out this little enterprise, as I have certain others, without bloodshed, but if I am compelled to use force, to resort to violence——"

The Thunderbolt did not have to conclude his threat. Francis Malberton gave a little cry of fear and dropped down lower in the big chair. His face was the color of ashes; he was the perfect picture of a man sorely afraid.

"That talk about being on the verge of bankruptcy is all right for the world at large, but you and I know the facts in the case," The Thunderbolt observed. "That box of bonds, for instance."

"I know of no box——"

Malberton ceased speaking as The Thunderbolt took another step toward him and raised the automatic pistol another inch or so, in order that the financier could look down the muzzle of it. Malberton gulped and licked at his lips again.

"Get up!" The Thunderbolt commanded.

It took Malberton a little time to get upon his feet. He was so weak from fright that he scarcely could stand. He swayed toward the table, put out a hand, and braced himself against it.

"Well?" he asked in a whisper.

"I am not going to trouble you to open that safe in the corner, Malberton, because there is little of value in it," The Thunderbolt declared. "But behind those panels in the other wall there is a second safe, in which I am deeply interested."

"You devil!" Malberton exclaimed. "How did you know that?"

"It is a part of my present business to know such things," The Thunderbolt told him. "And talk in whispers hereafter! Now lead the way to the safe!"

"Those bonds are all that I have left in the world," Malberton declared. "Even they belong to my creditors. You are going to leave me disgraced and penniless."

"I believe that we were to have an end of the comedy," The Thunderbolt observed. "To the safe! And let me drop one little hint—if by some means you manage to send in an alarm, and officers come to bother me, they'll find you dead or breathing your last when they enter!"

Francis Malberton almost collapsed. For, as he had lurched against the table, he had touched with the toe of one shoe a button concealed beneath the rug—a button that had flashed an alarm to police headquarters!

CHAPTER XIV

A HOT TRAIL

THE financier staggered toward the hidden safe. He was glad that his face was turned away from The Thunderbolt for the moment, for he feared that it would have betrayed him. Terror had shocked him until he moved more like a machine than a man. At first he seemed to be incapable of thinking.

He had sent in the alarm. The button and the connections with police headquarters formed Francis Malberton's only protection against thieves. He had installed that at the earnest solicitations of the other members of The Big Six, after the work of The Thunderbolt had commenced, and he had winced at the few dollars that it had cost him.

Now he found himself wishing that he had not spent those few dollars. He had touched the button mechanically, without stopping to think of the possible results. Malberton knew that a little red light had flashed up at police headquarters, that an operator there had given the alarm. Officers even now, perhaps, were on their way to the Malberton residence. They would surround it and probably enter to capture The Thunderbolt. But Francis Malberton

154

was afraid he would die before he could witness the capture.

He staggered on to the wall and touched a hidden spring, and two of the large panels separated and rolled back. Malberton had given up all hope of saving the bonds now. Perhaps he could have his life, though. If The Thunderbolt got the bonds quickly, perhaps he would leave the house quickly, get away before the police arrived. Then Malberton would be saved, though the bonds would be lost.

Even in that moment of terror Francis Malberton had an instant of satisfaction. He would not have to go ahead doctoring his books now. He could say that the bonds with which he had hoped to pay his creditors had been stolen. He could even mention an amount in excess of the value of the bonds, and so convert to his own use other assets. There was a gleam of comfort in the situation.

"Speed up!" The Thunderbolt commanded. "I do not want to be here until morning, you know!"

Malberton was ready and eager to speed up now. He wanted to get The Thunderbolt out of the house before the police arrived. He imagined that, if he did not, The Thunderbolt would strike him down with a single bullet. The Thunderbolt never had resorted to murder in his dealings with The Big Six, but that did not mean that he never would.

Malberton knelt before the door of the safe and began working at the combination. In his nervousness, his eagerness to get The Thunderbolt away, he made a mistake and was forced to begin again. His hands were shaking as he worked at the knob.

"Don't play for time," The Thunderbolt advised him in a whisper. "My trigger finger is liable to grow nervous, you know, if you keep me waiting too long."

Malberton made no reply. Heaven knew he was doing his best, working as swiftly as he could. And finally he pulled the door of the safe open and stood to one side.

"Take out the box," The Thunderbolt commanded.

Malberton took it out. As The Thunderbolt motioned, he carried it to the table.

"Unlock it!" The Thunderbolt ordered.

Malberton took a bunch of keys from his pocket, selected one quickly, and unlocked the box. Then The Thunderbolt motioned for him to stand back, and he did, against the wall. The Thunderbolt looked at the contents of the box. It seemed to Francis Malberton that he took a long time at it.

"A hundred thousand even," The Thunderbolt said, shutting the lid of the box again.

"And you'll leave me penniless," Malberton whined.

"As far as that is concerned——" The Thunderbolt began.

He stopped speaking suddenly. His head went up; he listened. From a distance, so faint that it scarcely could be heard, came the sound of whistling, a single bar of a popular song repeated over and over again.

The Thunderbolt whirled toward the financier.

"Sit down before that table!" he commanded. "And you stay there until I return!"

Francis Malberton dropped into the chair. He had not heard the whistling, and he did not know how to interpret The Thunderbolt's actions. He watched in fear and amazement as The Thunderbolt picked up the box of bonds, put it beneath his left arm, and darted to the hall door and opened it.

"Remember—don't move!" he commanded again.

And then he went on into the hall, silently, like a shadow, and Francis Malberton remained in the chair staring at the open door. He wanted to close that door and bolt it, to shout for help, to telephone the police, and ask whether the alarm had been observed. But he did not dare make a move.

The Thunderbolt hurried through the house and down into the basement. He reached the window through which he had gained entrance, and there he stopped. From a greater distance came the whistling again, but now the tune had been changed. The first had warned him—this told him that the house was surrounded. Saggs had done his work faithfully, and The Thunderbolt only hoped that he would do the rest as he had been ordered.

Back into the house he hurried, up the stairs to

the first floor, and crowded into a closet at one end of the hall. It was a tiny closet filled with old brooms, rags, cleaning preparations. The Thunderbolt found it a tight fit and knew that it would be hot, but he had no choice for the present. He closed the door upon himself and waited, his automatic held ready.

There was silence for a time. And then came the sharp ringing of a bell. The Thunderbolt guessed that it was the bell of the front door.

Francis Malberton had been sitting like a man stricken with paralysis. At the sound of the bell he sprang to his feet. His eyes were wide with terror. He remembered what The Thunderbolt had commanded and sank back into his chair again. The old manservant would hear that bell and answer it.

Again the bell pealed. Malberton licked at his dry lips and gripped the arms of the chair. Suddenly a burst of courage came to him. He got up and ran to the hall door. He snapped on the lights there. The Thunderbolt was not in sight. Malberton could hear the servant moving around on the upper floor preparing to answer the ring.

Malberton hurried through the hall to the door. He fumbled with lock and bolt, exclaiming wildly as he worked, and threw the door open. Detective Martin Radner stepped inside, another detective and a couple of policemen in uniform behind him.

Malberton gave a shout of delight and pawed at Radner's arm.

"The Thunderbolt!" he gasped. "He's been here——"

"We got the signal. How long ago?"

"He went just a minute before you rang the bell. He acted alarmed. Maybe he heard you coming."

Malberton was leading the way to the library as he spoke. Inside, he pointed to the open safe.

"He made me open it!" he cried. "He took a box —a box of bonds. They were intended for my creditors. I'm on the verge of bankruptcy. I want to get——"

Detective Martin Radner silenced him with a gesture. He did not care to hear the story of Francis Malberton's financial affairs at the moment. Here was a hot trail, if Malberton spoke the truth.

He darted to the telephone, and a moment later he had put in a call for the bloodhounds. He sent one of the officers outside to watch for their coming. And then he turned to Malberton again.

"Calm yourself and talk sense!" Radner ordered. "You have nothing to be afraid of now."

There was a wealth of sarcasm in the detective's voice, for Malberton was showing by every move and word what a craven he was. He dropped into the chair again, and Radner stood before him, his hands upon his hips.

"So he just got away?" he asked.

"Just a minute or so before the doorbell rang."

"How long had he been here?"

"I don't know. He frightened me so."

"What did he say and do? How did he get in?"

"I don't know that. I had a feeling that some-body was watching me, and I turned around. He was standing back near that corner, and he had a pistol in his——"

"Well, what did he do?"

"He threatened me. And then he forced me to open that safe, and he took the box of bonds. He seemed to know all about them—both the safe and the bonds. I—I didn't know that anybody knew about them, you see."

"What do you mean?"

"Why, that's a secret safe. See—there is another over there. He knew about that secret safe. And before I opened it he said that he had come to get the bonds. How he knew I had them, I cannot tell. I didn't think anybody knew."

"Buy them recently?"

"Yes," Malberton admitted. "My affairs are in a bad way. I've been caught in the market and squeezed. I had about enough to get out clean, I thought. So I turned my property into good bonds, picking them up cheap here and there, getting ready to turn them over so those I have to pay could get their money quickly."

"Buy them all in one place?"

"No—bought them wherever I could get them cheap, from men who needed money and had to sell at a sacrifice."

"And who do you think could learn about that safe and the bonds?" Radner wanted to know.

"I have no idea."

"What did The Thunderbolt look like?"

"He was tall. He wore the hood and had gloves on his hands. I couldn't tell much about him. And I was frightened——"

"I suppose so," Radner said. "How about his voice?"

"Very peculiar; sort of a monotone."

"Disguised, of course," said Radner. "We spoke once about young John Flatchley in connection with The Thunderbolt," Radner reminded him. "That was right after the second robbery. Remember? Well?"

"I couldn't say it was Flatchley, and I wouldn't say that it was not," Malberton declared. "His head and hands were covered——"

"Where did he go?"

"He went into the hall and turned toward the rear of the house. I didn't hear a sound after that. And now my bonds are gone. I'll not be able to pay those I owe——"

"You can take time to consider that later," Detective Radner told him coldly. "Just now the thing is to catch The Thunderbolt, if it is possible. And if he is the man we think, we have him!"

He turned toward the door as one of the uniformed officers hurried in from the hall.

"We've found where he got in, Radner," he reported. "There is a basement window open."

"Where is it?"

"Rear of the house," the officer replied.

Detective Radner showed sudden excitement. "Mr. Malberton, you wait here," he said.

He beckoned the officer to follow him and hurried outside and around to the open window. On the way he picked up another policeman who had not been to the rear of the residence.

"Smell anything unusual?" Radner asked this man.

"Something like perfume," the patrolman replied. "I got a whiff of it just as we came up."

"Great!" Radner exclaimed. "Great! I can't smell it, because I got my nostrils filled with it earlier in the evening. I think we've got Mr. Thunderbolt! I wish they'd hurry with those dogs."

"Perfume trail, or something like that?" one of the patrolmen asked.

"Exactly!" Detective Radner replied. "If he was the man I think, he has left behind him a trail that the dogs can follow easily. And if they do follow it, he'll have one hard time explaining, believe me!

And when the city learns the identity of The Thunderbolt—man! Talk about sensations!"

Detective Martin Radner was scarcely himself, and his brother officers noticed it and wondered. As a general thing Martin Radner did not indulge in enthusiasm. But thoughts of the possibility of catching The Thunderbolt caused him to forget his usual demeanor. Radner was enthusiastic to a great degree, and he did not care who knew it.

Suddenly he beckoned to one of the uniformed men.

"While we're waiting," he said, "it would be just as well to have a look through the house."

The man hurried out, but returned in a few minutes to say he had given the house a lookover and had found nothing.

When he had finished his report, the dogs arrived. There was a quick consultation, and then Detective Radner hurried into the house again, to find Malberton's old manservant with his master.

"We're taking the trail, Mr. Malberton, with dogs," Detective Radner reported. "You'd better shut that safe now. The Thunderbolt is done here, I fancy. And don't be frightened any more. We'll try to get back your bonds. It's all over as far as you are concerned, so try to breathe normally again. I'll let you know immediately if we catch him."

"But he threatened me!" Francis Malberton

gasped. "After you are gone, he may come back and kill me!"

"Not a chance of that!" Radner replied, laughing. "He is far from here, probably, and still going at a fair rate of speed. The Thunderbolt doesn't kill. He got the bonds he came for, and that settled it for him. But we are not done yet. He is liable to be disturbed before morning."

Detective Radner hurried from the house and around to the rear of the building, where the dogs were ready to take the trail. He left one patrolman at the front of the residence with orders to remain there half an hour or so, sent the other uniformed men back to their beats or the station house, and took the trail after the dogs with one other detective.

The dogs led the way to the alley and along it to the nearest street. They seemed to have no difficulty in following the scent. They turned up the avenue. Detective Martin Radner's eyes glistened. In that direction was the apartment house where John Flatchley had his suite.

CHAPTER XV

MALBERTON'S aged manservant had communicated to his wife the intelligence that The Thunderbolt had robbed their master, and she had returned to her bed because of a headache, and because she knew her husband could attend to Malberton in his fit of fright better than she could.

The financier had waved a hand weakly toward the carafe on the table, and the manservant poured him a glass of water and watched him gulp it down.

"This is terrible—terrible," Malberton said, moaning.

He began gathering up the papers on the table before him, putting them into bundles and wrapping twine around them. He staggered with them to the secret safe, locked them in, and returned the wall panels to their proper places.

Returning to the chair, Francis Malberton collapsed into it, while the servant stood by, waiting to be of what assistance he could.

"Terrible—terrible!" Malberton repeated and gasped.

"Can I get you anything, sir?"

165

"Nothing now. Wait a few minutes, and then I'll go up to bed. I wish they had left a lot of officers around the place. I'll never be able to sleep after this—never! I may as well——"

The servant, who was watching him closely, saw a look of horror come into his master's face, saw his eyes bulge, his lower jaw sag, his face turn from red to white. Francis Malberton began gasping like a dying man. His gaze of terror was directed across the room.

Instinctively the servant shivered as he turned his head. A little exclamation escaped his lips, but it was a very little one. And then he, too, leaned against the table with his eyes bulging and his breath coming in little gasps. For The Thunderbolt stood there in the doorway, his automatic held ready.

"I never signaled the police—— I never——" Malberton began mouthing in a hoarse whisper.

"Of course you did, but what of it?" The Thunderbolt asked. "I am not going to shoot you just now, you coward. You're a brave man when it comes to stealing money from widows and orphans and clerks and stenographers, but you're not much of a man when you meet another man face to face, are you?"

"Where did you come from? I thought—— They were after you——"

"They are chasing away across the city, I believe, on some sort of silly trail," The Thunderbolt said. "I simply hid in a closet and waited until they had gone. You see, I had not concluded my business with you."

"You got the bonds——"

"Oh, yes, I got the bonds," The Thunderbolt acknowledged. "But that was only half of it, you see."

"So you're going to kill me!"

"I may, if you don't talk in whispers," The Thunderbolt said. "I'd hate to waste a cartridge on you, but if I were forced——"

"What do you want, then?"

"Another box."

"What do you mean?"

"You have an old box lined with purple plush," The Thunderbolt told him.

"Yes. An old thing that has been in the family for generations," the financier replied, his eyes bulging again. "I keep a few trinkets in it—a few bits of old-fashioned jewelry that belonged to my mother. Surely you don't want that?"

"I do not make a practice of stealing heirlooms, especially when they are worth but a few dollars," The Thunderbolt said. "However, I think I'd better take a look at the box."

"But it is valueless——"

"And I am not inclined to waste much time about it," The Thunderbolt interrupted.

He took a step forward and raised the automatic.

Malberton shrank back into the chair, and the aged servant gave a gasp of terror.

"I—I'll get it!" Malberton said.

He got out of the chair and staggered across the room to the safe—the old safe this time, the one in plain sight. Kneeling before it, he worked the combination. He opened the safe and took out the old box and carried it back to the table.

"Nothing but some old-fashioned jewelry that wouldn't bring a hundred dollars," he muttered. "Surely you can leave me these few keepsakes when you have already taken a fortune in bonds."

"Open it!" The Thunderbolt commanded.

Francis Malberton touched a little catch and opened the box. It was not even locked.

"Just a few keepsakes——" the financier whispered.

"Do you take me for an idiot?" The Thunderbolt asked. "Do you think I would be here now, risking liberty, if there was nothing in that box except a few keepsakes?"

"There—you can see."

"I see the keepsakes," The Thunderbolt said. "And I see, also, that the box has a rather thick bottom. Suppose, Mr. Malberton, that you cease wasting time and open the secret bottom of the box."

"What?" Malberton cried.

"Did you think nobody knew your secret?" The

Thunderbolt asked. "Faced with ruin, because of a swindle, knowing you would have to make restitution, you planned to swindle your victims further—and fool the courts, also. I have been watching you for some time, Malberton. You got rid of all your property except this old house and a few worthless vacant lots. You turned the money into bonds, and you were ready to make away with them, then go into bankruptcy, get cleared, and then unearth the bonds and live like a king on them. But I got the bonds!"

"Yes, but these keepsakes——"

"Oh, you didn't put all your money in bonds," The Thunderbolt said. "You were afraid that they might be discovered or traced, and that you'd be forced to disgorge them. So you bought, here and there, unset diamonds."

"You—you——" Malberton cried.

"Keep your voice down, please! You bought unset gems, and you put them into the bottom of that old box. You expected to get away with that box no matter what happened. But you are not going to, Mr. Malberton. Open the bottom of the box."

"No, no! They're all I have!"

"Open the box!" The Thunderbolt repeated.

His eyes glittered through the slits in the hood; the automatic was raised again until it covered Malberton's heart. The menace was more than Malberton could endure. He gave a sob, touched a spring, and the false bottom of the box flew open.

Even the old servant gasped his surprise. There in the false bottom, on the purple plush, were scintillating stones that caught the light and flashed it back in flakes of flame.

The Thunderbolt chuckled. "Unset, and easy to market," he said. "This is a good night's work for me, Malberton. And now you are broke, as you would have persons believe."

"Who are you?" Malberton cried, whirling toward him. "How did you know?"

"I have been watching you, I said. I knew of your crooked deal, and knew that you'd be caught, that there would be an attempt made on the part of your dupes to force restitution. When you began disposing of good income-bearing property at the market I began watching closer. I knew you were buying bonds, knew that you were buying unset stones."

"But how did you know where I was keeping them?" Malberton's curiosity was getting the better of his fear.

"On four different nights," replied The Thunderbolt, "I watched you as you sat at this table. I watched from that window in the corner. The shade is an inch short. It might have paid you, Malberton, if you had bought a new shade for that window. I saw you put diamonds in this box. A

man always feels secure in his own house, and
grows careless. That is what you did, Malberton.
I don't want the old box—but I'll take the diamonds."

Malberton whimpered. The Thunderbolt took another step forward. But there came a voice from
the door.

"That's far enough! Put 'em up!"

The Thunderbolt whirled. In the hall door stood
a patrolman, his revolver held ready for instant use.

"So you watched him through the window, did
you?" the excited and elated officer said. "Good
enough! I watched you from the same place and
came in to take a hand in the game. Radner left
me around here for half an hour or so, and it was
a good thing. Where Radner has chased to I don't
know—but you're *my* meat, Mr. Thunderbolt!"

"Am I?" The Thunderbolt asked.

"And I'll plug you the first move you make!" the
patrolman said. "So don't try any tricks! Drop
that automatic! Drop it!"

The Thunderbolt hesitated a moment and then
dropped the weapon. It struck the rug at Malberton's feet.

"Kick it this way, Mr. Malberton," the patrolman
ordered.

The financier, still shaking with terror, managed
to kick the automatic at least off the rug, where The
Thunderbolt could not get it quickly.

"You and your servant get those cords off the portières, while I keep an eye on this bird," the officer ordered next. "Be quick about it! We'll get him securely bound, and then we'll strip off that hood and see what The Thunderbolt looks like. Get the cords!"

Malberton and the servant hurried across the room to get them, both trembling, both wondering what would happen to the policeman who had dared confront The Thunderbolt. But a uniform has a strong appeal, and Malberton began to lose some of his fear.

Yet the capture of The Thunderbolt would not be to his advantage, Malberton realized. He did not know how much of the low conversation the policeman had heard. He was afraid that he would not be able to save his diamonds, if the fact was known that he possessed them, but perhaps he could arrange to keep some of them for himself. And if he could get hold of that box of bonds he could remove at least a share of them before the box was turned over to his creditors.

He fumbled with the cords, the old servant trying to help him, both of them so nervous that they scarcely could unfasten the knots and get the cords loose. The policeman did not remove his glance from The Thunderbolt; and The Thunderbolt stood straight in front of the table, his hands raised above his head, his eyes glittering through the slits in his hood. He made no move; he did not attempt to speak a word.

But he was doing a great deal of rapid thinking. He was remembering that, to the world at large, he was John Flatchley, scion of a well-known and highly-respected family, and that his capture would mean instant disgrace, perhaps a long term in prison, and the broken heart of Agnes Larimer!

He watched the policeman closely, and once he glanced quickly toward the doorway where Malberton and the servant were getting the cords. The policeman seemed to be a man of some brains, and unusually watchful. The Thunderbolt supposed that it was because of the big rewards that had been offered for his capture.

He must prevent the capture, he told himself. This was a crisis where a great effort had to be made. It was better to run a risk than to stand effortless and allow them to bind his arms and legs and carry him away to police headquarters. No man ever must look behind the hood of The Thunderbolt and find the countenance of John Flatchley.

One thing the policeman in the doorway did not know—The Thunderbolt had another automatic in a sling beneath his left arm, inside his coat. The coat was not buttoned now, but there was danger for The Thunderbolt in making a sudden move for the pistol. The policeman refused to grow careless even for the necessary fraction of a second.

"My arms are tired!" The Thunderbolt said suddenly, in a hoarse voice.

"I suppose so," the policeman assented. "Well, lower the elbows a few inches and rest them, but don't make any other sort of move, unless you're eager to end things without a trial."

The Thunderbolt lowered his elbows. That made things a bit better, but they were not good enough yet. And now the trembling Francis Malberton and his servant had unfastened the cords and were advancing across the room.

"Here they are," Malberton said.

"Good enough!" the policeman replied. "Go over and tie his feet together first. Be sure to tie them well. And then we'll lower his arms and lash them behind him, and then we'll take off that hood and have a look at his face. His feet first. He has a record for speed, and I'd like to see him live up to it with his feet tied."

"I—— Perhaps you'd better do it," Malberton said.

"Do it yourself—you and your servant," the policeman said. "I am going to stand right here ready for business until those feet are tied. We've got The Thunderbolt, and we want to keep him. Hurry with the work!"

Francis Malberton shuddered as he looked at The Thunderbolt and caught the ominous glitter of his eyes. But he went across the room with the servants at his heels, and approached the prisoner, holding the cords awkwardly.

"Go to it!" the policeman commanded. "He won't make any funny moves while I've got him covered."

Malberton seemed to have a moment of courage. He hurried to The Thunderbolt's side, and the servant went around the table and to the other side. Malberton tossed a cord behind The Thunderbolt, and both he and the servant knelt to wrap it around the prisoner's legs and tie it there.

The Thunderbolt knew that now was the time to act. If he delayed a few seconds longer it would be too late. And suddenly he decided to make a move. He sprang backward and dropped. He pushed Francis Malberton in front of him, shoved the servant to one side. At the same instant the policeman fired, but the shot went over The Thunderbolt's head and crashed into the wall.

He held the second shot, for The Thunderbolt had acted with a speed engendered by the crisis. The latter had whipped the automatic from beneath his left arm, one sheet of flame had come from it, and the single incandescent light over the table had ceased its usefulness.

The room was in darkness. The Thunderbolt kicked at the servant again and caused him to howl with pain. He tossed Malberton aside. The policeman was confronted with half a dozen noises in the dark and dared not fire for fear of hitting Malberton or the servant.

Quickly The Thunderbolt's hand went up, and he got the old plush box. The diamonds were scooped out; they found their way into one of The Thunderbolt's pockets. And then he crept swiftly to the wall and along it to the door.

"Turn on the lights, Malberton—quick!" the policeman cried. "Aren't there any more? Speak—let me know where you are!"

But Francis Malberton found himself stricken momentarily dumb. He was afraid to speak, afraid that The Thunderbolt was near him, would hear him and locate him, and take a terrible revenge. The servant groaned.

"Where are you, Malberton?" the policeman cried again.

Then a flash of light split the darkness. The officer had his electric torch out. It revealed the servant and Malberton. And before the policeman could sweep it the rest of the way over the room a blow descended upon him, and he groaned and toppled forward, the torch going out. The Thunderbolt had struck once with the butt of the automatic, and he had struck the proper spot. The policeman would not take an interest in events for several minutes.

Into the hall The Thunderbolt dashed silently. He got the box of bonds from the closet and went on into the basement. Through the window he crawled, and for a moment he crouched at the side of the house to make sure that there were no officers there. Then he darted across the rear lawn to the alley.

Through the dark alley he hurried to the nearest street. In the last patch of darkness he removed his hood and gloves and stowed them away in the pockets meant for them. Then, with the box of bonds beneath his arm, he hurried up the street, keeping to the shadows as much as possible, watching ahead for pedestrians. He did not care to be recognized.

He came to a small park and hurried across it beneath the trees. Now he came to a boulevard that was in almost total darkness save at the street intersections. Along it he hurried, and presently he turned into another alley and crept along close to a high brick wall. He came to a gate, stopped for a moment to listen, and then opened the gate and slipped inside another rear yard.

He did not stop to rest, for this thing had been timed closely, and he had lost some time at the Malberton house because of the policeman. Once more he adjusted his hood and gloves; once more he crept to the rear of a residence.

It was the home of the district attorney!

CHAPTER XVI

SURRENDERED LOOT

THE district attorney was a vigorous man physically and mentally; he was one of the tribe who use sleeping porches. The Thunderbolt had taken the trouble to ascertain a great many things about the district attorney. He knew that his bedchamber could be entered easily, and the sleeping porch extended from it; also that the servants in the house slept on the third floor in the rear; also that the district attorney's wife, and his daughter of twenty, slept in another wing in apartments lavishly furnished.

For the district attorney was a wealthy man, and had been all his life. Despite that fact he had applied himself to the law like a penniless student and had worked as hard to succeed. He filled his office with care, though he could have lived an easy life with no worries at all.

Secure in his own position, the district attorney could not be influenced by wealthy men, and his work had been impartial and fair. The Thunderbolt banked a great deal on that now. As John Flatchley, The Thunderbolt knew the district attorney well.

178

They belonged to the same clubs and often played golf together. But The Thunderbolt had no fear of being recognized.

The Thunderbolt made his entrance through a window that had been left open a few inches. Inside, he stopped for a moment to listen and then went silently across the room to the door that opened into the sleeping porch.

Behind his hood The Thunderbolt grinned. The district attorney was stretched on his back, snoring; he made anything but a dignified picture. Beside the head of the bed was a little table, and on the table were documents and a little reading light still burning. The Thunderbolt guessed that the district attorney had dropped asleep without turning off the light.

Stepping to the side of the bed The Thunderbolt shook the official roughly. The district attorney grunted and opened his eyes, rubbed at them with his fists, and then sat up in the bed, startled rather than afraid.

"Take it easy!" The Thunderbolt advised. "No harm is coming to you unless you attempt to cause harm to me."

"Who——"

"I am The Thunderbolt. I dare say you have heard of me?"

The district attorney had. He grunted his surprise again and started to get out of the bed

"As you were!" The Thunderbolt told him. "Kindly remain seated, sir, and listen. I have not come to rob you."

"Um!" the district attorney grunted.

But the sleep was out of his eyes now, and he realized his situation. He watched The Thunderbolt closely, but The Thunderbolt was standing back a short distance, and the reading light did not reveal him well. The district attorney knew better than to adjust the light.

"Well, what is it?" he asked snappily.

"You are not talking to your office boy," The Thunderbolt said chuckling. "Pay attention to what I have to say, for it will be food for thought, and undoubtedly it will please you."

"I'm listening."

"And sit as you are, without moving," The Thunderbolt warned. "I came here to do you a favor, and it would not be nice if you tried to shoot me or call the police."

"Well?"

"You know Francis Malberton, one of The Big Six, of course?"

"Yes. Go on."

"Malberton has perpetrated another swindle, and this time he was not careful. A howl has been raised. He will be forced to make restitution."

"I know all about it—have been investigating it."

"Good enough!" said The Thunderbolt. "For

some time past Malberton has been disposing of property and making false entries on his books. With a great deal of the money he purchased negotiable bonds. It was his intention to hide these bonds and go through bankruptcy, claiming that his fortune had gone in bad speculation. His creditors would get very little, and after the court discharged him he would have the bonds, you see."

"This is interesting," the district attorney said.

"A short time ago I got the bonds!"

"You stole them from Malberton?"

"I did. They are in this box—a hundred thousand dollars' worth of them. I am going to leave them with you."

"What's the idea?"

"I want his poor dupes to get a share of their money back," The Thunderbolt replied. "I leave these bonds here, and you can do with them as you please. Of course, you will know officially that Malberton has this much, and cannot hide them now. He would not be able to make an explanation."

"Great!" the district attorney said. "I've been after that swindler for some time, but never could get my hands on him. But I don't understand this. How does it happen that you are so altruistic? Why not keep the bonds for yourself?"

"Oh, I got mine! Malberton had a large quantity of unset diamonds, too, and I am keeping those. But you can have the bonds and force Malberton to give them to his dupes."

"I'll do that, all right. But I am not in the habit of making deals with crooks," the district attorney said. "I admire this act of yours, but you are a criminal, wanted by the authorities, and——"

"And you'd nab me if you could," The Thunderbolt interrupted. "But you can't. If you make a wrong move we'll lose an eminent district attorney."

"You've never killed yet, it is said."

"Perhaps because I have not been forced to do so," The Thunderbolt replied. "And you are not sure that I'd not if circumstance compelled me. So you are going to behave and do exactly as I say."

"You seem quite sure of it."

"I am," The Thunderbolt replied.

"I notice that you talk like a man of some culture."

"Not all criminals are illiterate," The Thunderbolt observed. "I'd like to remain here for a time and talk with you; since you are a well-educated man yourself, but it is time I should be going. I've done what I came to do. Here is the box of bonds on the floor."

"And now what?" the district attorney asked.

"Now you are to get out of bed, holding your hands above your head, and follow me into this room adjoining."

The district attorney did so, and The Thunderbolt

watched him carefully and menaced him with the automatic. The Thunderbolt backed through the doorway, and the district attorney followed at a distance of a few feet.

"Stop there!" The Thunderbolt ordered suddenly. "I can see you plainly because of the light on the sleeping porch, but you cannot see me very well. I am going back to the window and get through it. It is quite dark outside. As soon as I am gone you may make all the noise you please. But not a move until I go!"

He darted swiftly to the window through which he had entered the house, and there he stood for a moment, while the district attorney remained in the doorway, his hands held high above his head.

"Officially I'd like to put my hands on you," the district attorney said. "But personally I hope you get away."

"Oh, I'll get away!"

"If you must steal, confine your efforts to high-class swindlers, as you have been doing."

"I intend to do so," The Thunderbolt said.

The district attorney could hear him chuckling again. And then The Thunderbolt dropped suddenly through the window and ran. The district attorney hurried across the room. Outside was the black night. He could not tell in which direction The Thunderbolt had gone.

Out in the alley and safe, The Thunderbolt removed his hood and gloves once more and stowed them away. Then he hurried on to the street.

He had a distance of four blocks to go before he could reach home. And he knew that he was a bit later than he should have been. He had been delayed by the policeman at Malberton's, and he had talked too long with the district attorney. He wondered whether Saggs had carried out all his orders carefully, whether Saggs had reached home.

Once he was obliged to dart inside a yard and crouch against the bole of a tree because a patrolman was coming along the street. The Thunderbolt did not wish to be seen without his hood. He did not want it known that John Flatchley had left his rooms after returning to them, following the silver wedding reception.

After the patrolman had passed The Thunderbolt went into the street again and hurried the remainder of the distance. He turned into the alley and approached the rear of the apartment house. From the alley he could not see whether the lights were on in his rooms.

He went through the tradesmen's entrance and hurried to the dumb-waiter. Into it he crawled and reached for the knot of rope at the bottom, that served as a cable. He pulled in a bit of slack and tugged, and the dumb-waiter commenced moving upward.

Presently he came to his own apartment. The

door of the dumb-waiter shaft was open an inch or
so.   The Thunderbolt slipped out, closed the door,
and hurried across the dark kitchenette.   Into the
hall he went and stopped at the door of a room.

"Saggs!" he whispered sharply.

The door was opened immediately.

"Here, boss!" Saggs said.

"How long have you been home?"

"Almost an hour.   Gosh, boss, you had me worried!   I never knew you to be late before.   I was
afraid——"

"Undressed?"

"In my pajamas, boss."

"Good.   If we are paid a visit——"

He ceased speaking.   In the front hall a buzzer
sounded.   Some one was at the door.

CHAPTER XVII

CREAM OF THE JEST

"THE door, Saggs!" The Thunderbolt whispered. "Don't go for a couple of minutes, and stall until I show up."

"All right, boss."

The Thunderbolt darted into his own bedroom and snapped on a small light. He glanced first at the bed. Good Saggs! Saggs had taken the trouble to muss up that bed so it would look as though a man had been sleeping there.

Not a second was lost. The Thunderbolt stripped off his clothes and put them in a receptacle beneath the floor, the existence of which even Saggs did not know. The diamonds remained in the pocket of the coat. The hood, the gloves, the automatic, and the electric torch went into the hole also.

And then The Thunderbolt got into his pajamas with a speed that would have made a metropolitan fireman green with envy. He darted to the dressing table and looked into the mirror. He mussed his hair, dusted white powder over his face quickly, and as quickly wiped it off.

Saggs had answered the third ring of the buzzer.

He opened the door on a crack and peered out. Detective Martin Radner stood there, with another officer at his back. Saggs knew him by sight, but Radner did not know Saggs.

"Mr. Flatchley's room?" Radner asked.

"Yes, sir."

"I am an officer," Radner said, showing his shield. "Who are you?"

"Mr. Flatchley's valet, sir."

"Is Mr. Flatchley in?"

"Why, yes, sir!" said Saggs. "He is in bed, sir."

"I want to see him."

"But, sir——" Saggs protested.

At that moment John Flatchley opened the door of his bedroom and stood in it, yawning.

"What is it, Saggs?" he asked.

"An officer, sir."

"Let him in, Saggs."

"Yes, sir," said Saggs. He stepped back and bowed, and Radner and the other detective stepped through the short hall and into the big living room.

There stood John Flatchley, in his pajamas, yawning, his hair rumpled, his eyes evidently heavy with sleep. Radner could look through the open door and see the bed, with the covers thrown back and the pillows mussed.

"Detective Radner!" Flatchley exclaimed. "What brings you here at this unearthly hour?"

"We were passing the place, and I thought I saw

somebody climbing up to your balcony," Radner said. "I thought possibly you were having a visit from a burglar."

Flatchley felt like laughing at the other's clumsy explanation of the call, but he did not.

"Heavens!" he gasped. "Saggs, turn on all the lights, and we'll take a look around."

"Yes, sir," said Saggs.

And when the lights were on, John Flatchley led the way, and they went entirely through the apartment, Detective Martin Radner with his eyes very much open. But the detective saw nothing that aroused his suspicion.

"Must have been mistaken," he grunted, when they had returned to the living room.

"Glad you aroused us, at any rate," Flatchley replied. "Shows that the police are on the job. Saggs, get the gentlemen some refreshments and cigars."

Saggs went back to the kitchenette to get what had been ordered. Safe behind the door, he grinned. He opened a bottle of grape juice and got out some glasses and a box of cigars and even a plate of sandwiches that had been intended for Flatchley himself. He carried the tray to the living room and put it on the table, then hurried for Mr. Flatchley's dressing gown, helped him into it, and excused himself and retired. But he listened from behind the door of the bedroom.

"The Thunderbolt has been at work again," Detective Martin Radner said, watching Flatchley closely as he munched at a sandwich.

"Indeed? What has the fellow done this time?"

"He got at Francis Malberton."

"Robbed old Malberton, eh?" Flatchley said. "Well, he can spare it, I suppose."

"I don't know. Malberton made a howl to me that he was about broke. The Thunderbolt got a box filled with perfectly good bonds."

"Nothing small about the fellow," Flatchley said.

"And we trailed him—with dogs."

"Um! Catch him?"

"Not yet," said Radner, his face flushing.

"You don't mean to say that you trailed the beggar to this neighborhood?"

"We did not, no! It was a peculiar trail, too. The dogs trailed easily, because of a perfume The Thunderbolt had on."

"Perfume? Imagine that!"

"It was a queer trail," Detective Radner admitted. "It led us a couple of miles up and down streets and across lawns. Once it approached the home of another rich man, and we thought maybe we'd catch The Thunderbolt working there. But just before it reached the house the trail went away again, down another street, and across a couple of vacant lots."

"The Thunderbolt must be a pedestrian," Flatchley commented.

"We came to the end of the trail finally, at the entrance to a house."

"And you didn't catch him?"

"We did not!" Radner said. "The trail ended there. But The Thunderbolt was not there. And then we discovered that we had not been trailing him at all."

"How is that?"

"I telephoned headquarters, and I found that The Thunderbolt had paid a second visit to Malberton after we had taken the trail. He got a bunch of unset diamonds the second trip. And one of our men almost got him, but The Thunderbolt played some trick and got away. And after that he paid a visit to the district attorney—only a short time ago. The district attorney had just informed headquarters when I phoned."

"Fancy a crook paying a visit to the district attorney!" Flatchley said. "Radner, this Thunderbolt is too clever for you!"

"Think so?" Radner said, as if he snarled the words. "He's clever, I'll admit. But I'll get him yet."

"Be a feather in your cap if you do," Flatchley commented. "Some reward, too, I understand."

"I'll get him!" Radner declared again. "He played some sort of trick on me to-night. He had help, too. But I'll get him—and don't you forget it!"

"Please me to read about it in the papers when you do," Flatchley said. "Have another sandwich?"

But Detective Radner did not care for another sandwich. He left with his comrade almost at once. As Saggs reappeared in the living room again The Thunderbolt put finger to lips to command silence. He suspected Detective Martin Radner of listening just outside the door.

"What do you think of that, Saggs?" The Thunderbolt said in tones loud enough to be heard in the hall. "Robbed Mr. Malberton! Got bonds and diamonds! This Thunderbolt chap has nerve, Saggs."

"Yes, sir," Saggs said.

"He goes around gathering fortunes with ease, it seems to me. I certainly hope he doesn't visit us, Saggs. I haven't a great deal, but I'd hate to lose what I have."

"Certainly, sir," said Saggs.

"Think I'll go back to bed. Was having a good sleep, confound it! What time is it, Saggs?"

"Four o'clock, sir."

"Then you let me sleep this morning—understand? I've got a golf match this afternoon with the district attorney."

"Yes, sir," Saggs said.

The Thunderbolt passed into the bedroom, and Saggs snapped out the living-room lights and followed, closing the door carefully. The Thunderbolt was sitting on the side of the bed, chuckling.

"Saggs, that was great!" he said, in a whisper. "Got home just in time, didn't I?"

"You sure did, boss. I was scared stiff for a time. If you'd been half an hour later——"

"But I wasn't. Our luck still holds. You should see the diamonds I got, Saggs. When they are marketed they'll go a long way toward refunding the victims of The Big Six. One more man on our list, Saggs, and then our work is done."

"You sure had me worried, boss."

"And now I want a report from you. I didn't catch all of it from what Radner said. I told you to make a long trail, and end it in front of the house of some respectable citizen."

"And I sure obeyed orders, boss," Saggs said.

"Well, tell me about it!"

"After you'd got into that Malberton house, boss, I put on those shoes and trailed from the basement window to a tree about halfway to the alley wall. I got up into the tree. I could see up and down the alley and watch the few light spots, and I could see out into the street."

"Ah, a good position of advantage."

"Sure," said Saggs. "And there I waited and watched. And I was sure surprised to see the cops sneakin' up on the house."

"It surprised me, too. Old Malberton must have touched off some sort of alarm."

"So I gave you the signal, boss, and then kept

quiet in the tree. They crept up and surrounded the house, and then I slipped down from the tree and got into the alley, and slipped along that to the street. Then I went ahead and made the trail. I knew I'd have plenty of time. Radner would have to telephone for the dogs."

"Certainly," said The Thunderbolt.

"But it worried me, boss, because I knew you didn't have time to get out of the home. I was hopin' that you'd be able to hide where they wouldn't find you, and get out after they put the dogs on the trail."

"Which is precisely what I did, Saggs. Great minds run in the same channel."

"So I went ahead makin' the trail, boss. I went up one street and down another, and cut across lots and through alleys, and fussed around in a park a while. I certainly fixed up a hot trail for those dogs, and I knew I was goin' faster than they could follow."

"And where did you lead them, Saggs?"

"I remembered what you had said, boss. So I went to the mayor's house, but turned away just before I got there. And then I went to within a block of police headquarters and turned away again."

The Thunderbolt chuckled. "That must have puzzled our friend Radner," he said.

"He ain't any friend of mine. And then I came

back into this part of town, boss, and circled away from the boulevard toward the west."

"Good boy!"

"I thought it was about time to quit, then, and that maybe that perfume stuff would be gettin' cold. So I hurried to the place I had in mind, went right to the side door, and there I sat down and took off my shoes, rewrapped them carefully, and put on the others I was carryin'. Then I took out that little squirter thing and squirted ammonia over the bottoms of my trousers, like you said. And then I got away from there and hurried home."

"Good job, too!" The Thunderbolt commented. "A merry jest—and Detective Martin Radner is worried stiff over it. I have an idea that he still suspects me. A good joke! But whose house did you end the trail at, Saggs?"

"Why, it was the house of the chief of police," Saggs said, grinning.

The Thunderbolt threw back his head and laughed, dropped back on the bed, and crushed his face into a pillow; Saggs could see his shoulders heaving.

This continued for nearly a minute, and then The Thunderbolt controlled his merriment and sat up again.

"Great work!" he said. "The cream of the jest. If our last little adventure is as successful I'll be grateful."

CHAPTER XVIII

UNDER SURVEILLANCE

THE chief blew a cloud of tobacco smoke toward the ceiling of his private office, glanced across the room at Detective Martin Radner, and spoke.

"The newspapers," said the chief, "are commencing to intimate that 'The Thunderbolt' is getting 'protection.' You know what that means, Radner. Another week of it, and they'll be coming out openly and accusing us of graft. And then his honor, the mayor, will feel inclined to ask for a few resignations in the police department, starting with me and possibly getting as far down the line as you. There'll be a great shake-up, sensations, and all that. Confound it, can't we do something? Isn't it possible to save our own skins and put The Thunderbolt in jail?"

Detective Martin Radner threw wide his arms in a gesture meant to indicate utter despair. Then he thrust his hands far down in the pockets of his trousers, cocked his head to one side, chewed furiously at his unlighted cigar, and began pacing back and forth from corner to corner of the chief's private office again.

195

"Chief," he said, after a time, coming to a stop at one end of the big desk, "I know all about the newspapers and the mayor. And I don't blame them, don't blame anybody for anything! We're a poor lot!"

"What?"

"When it comes to apprehending criminals and putting them where they belong, we're about as good as a year-old baby trying to make a political speech. As for me—I'm ready to admit that I'm a broken-down, cracked, bruised, and battered old man who ought to be in some charitable institution. I'm a has-been or a never-was, I don't know which. Why, dang it, I ought to be ashamed to draw my salary every month. I——"

The chief raised one hand by way of protest. "Oh, I don't think it is that bad!" he said. "We have been unsuccessful, that's all. The Thunderbolt has us going—but we're not necessarily gone. We'll get him yet!"

"I haven't much hope," Detective Radner admitted.

"You've got a moment of pessimism, that's all," the chief said. "We've got to get him, Radner! That last stunt of his makes laughingstocks of us. And The Big Six——"

"The Big Six!" Detective Radner sneered. "Just between ourselves, chief, The Thunderbolt ought to be given a medal for robbing The Big Six."

"Yes, I know," the chief said. "They are a proper bunch of high-class financial crooks, and nothing less, but they happen to be the six most influential men in our fair city. And they have been robbed."

"Five of them have," Radner corrected. "William Granner has escaped, so far."

"And you think that he'll be the next victim of The Thunderbolt?" the chief asked.

"I'm willing to make a bet that he'll be the next!" the detective said. "He is as good as robbed right now."

"All jokes aside, Radner, what do you think of the situation, and what are you doing about it?" the chief asked. "I gave you a free hand, you will remember, and told you to ask me for any help you wanted."

"I know it, chief. And I've fallen down—hard! Chief, I'm still of the opinion that The Thunderbolt is young John Flatchley—clubman, social pet, general swell—and not a regular criminal at all."

"Rats!"

"Uh-huh! You say 'rats!' I don't!"

"Well, what are you doing about it now? What arrangements have you made?" the chief asked. "I suppose you've investigated him fully?"

"I've had him watched—done everything," Detective Radner replied. "William Granner is the only one of The Big Six who has not been robbed.

So I have half a dozen good men watching Granner and his valuables. We're guarding his office and house night and day."

"Good!" the chief grunted.

"And I am having John Flatchley watched night and day, too. If The Thunderbolt makes an attempt to rob Granner we should land him, whether he is John Flatchley or not. I'm using a lot of men, chief, but we've got to get him if he tries to work on Granner. If we don't get him then, we may never hear of The Thunderbolt again—especially if he is Flatchley."

"Good enough!" the chief exclaimed. "I don't know what more you can do. Well, I hope that you land him, Radner! If he robs William Granner and makes his get-away, we may as well start looking around for new jobs."

"I'm having that valet of Flatchley's watched, too, just on the chance that he might know something," Detective Radner continued. "And we are watching all the known crooks who happen to be in town, and looking out for all the suspicious strangers. It's quite some job, but we'll keep it up for a couple of months if it is necessary, if The Thunderbolt does not make some sort of move before the end of that time."

"Good!" the chief repeated. "You do whatever you wish, Radner—but get The Thunderbolt!"

Detective Martin Radner bobbed his head by way

of answer and strode from the chief's private office, his hands still in his pockets, his unlighted cigar a mass of tobacco pulp between his teeth.

Saggs stood in a corner of the living room of John Flatchley's suite, bending forward and glancing through the window at the street below. He made a peculiar noise deep down in his throat. The noise represented nothing so much as disgust, anger, and mingled fear, a sort of queer combination calculated to cause a peculiar noise in a man's throat.

As he turned away from the window Saggs looked quickly around the room. He snapped off a light, turned on another, adjusted the evening paper on one end of the long table, patted a couple of cushions into place, and then was satisfied that everything was as John Flatchley wished it.

It was about half past five o'clock in the afternoon, but the day had been a gray one, and it was dark in the apartment without the lights. Saggs tried to tell himself that the gloomy day had affected him, but he knew better. He felt like a fish caught in a net, he told himself.

Saggs made no attempt to deny to himself that he was nervous. He wished that John Flatchley would come home, though he knew that Flatchley was dining out that evening at the home of Agnes Larimer and so would return soon to dress.

He walked across the room to the window again,

and once more he glanced down at the street. Just opposite, in a doorway, stood a man dressed indifferently, puffing at a pipe, the picture of a loafer waiting for a friend.

But Saggs knew that he was not an ordinary loafer—he was a member of the city police department, attached to the detective bureau. Saggs could tell a detective or plain-clothes man as far as he could see one.

Then Saggs suddenly rejoiced, for a motor car drew up before the big bachelor apartment house, and John Flatchley stepped out and turned for an instant to give the chauffeur some directions. Then he turned and entered the building briskly.

Quickly Saggs looked around the apartment again, to make sure that everything was as it should be. He hurried into the little hall, so he would be able to open the door the instant that John Flatchley's finger touched the buzzer button. It was no fear of losing a job that got this close attention from Saggs. He worshiped John Flatchley and was always eager to serve him.

The buzzer sounded. Saggs opened the door, John Flatchley entered, and Saggs took his hat, coat, gloves, and stick. Flatchley went into the living room, dropped into a chair, and lighted a cigarette. His valet hovered around in the background, eager, anxious, but knowing that he must wait until John Flatchley saw fit to engage him in conversation

He did not have to wait long.

"Saggs!"

"Yes, sir."

"Do you happen to notice any sort of change taking place in me, Saggs?"

"No, sir."

"Nevertheless, Saggs, I am changing. Watch closely! Ah—I no longer am John Flatchley, Saggs —now I am The Thunderbolt!"

The little comedy that they always played being over, Saggs changed also, and instead of a valet he became a sort of comrade-in-arms.

"Gosh, boss, I'm glad that you pulled that change so quick!" Saggs said. "I'm so full of information that I'm almost ready to bust!"

"Ah! A few little annoyances this afternoon, Saggs, or something like that?"

"Yeh! They came around here inspectin' the electric wirin' this afternoon, boss—lookin' for a short circuit, they said. That wasn't what they were lookin' for, of course."

"I suppose not, Saggs."

"They pried around considerable, boss, but a fat lot of good it did them. One of the men was an electrician, all right—probably a city electrician. The other was a joke. He might as well have worn his shield on the outside of his overalls, boss. I spotted him the minute I saw him."

Flatchley grinned. "Detective?" he asked.

"I suppose he draws a detective's pay," Saggs replied with a great deal of sarcasm in his voice. "If you're askin' me, he couldn't detect an elephant in a circus parade."

" 'Um! Did they go away satisfied?"

"I don't know about that, boss. They messed around the kitchen and tapped around the floors and walls like they were tryin' to find a hollow place."

John Flatchley grinned again. "They didn't find one, eh?" he said.

"I guess not, boss."

"Nevertheless, there is a dandy hollow space, and even you do not know just where it is," Flatchley said. "I didn't think they'd locate it. Anything else, Saggs?"

"There's a yap across the street watchin' the windows, of course. There's been one there for a week, day and night. And there's another in the alley."

"Quite interesting!" John Flatchley observed. "There was one at my club this afternoon, too."

"Boss, that Radner man is after us hot and heavy again, if you're askin' me!"

"What if he is?"

"Sometimes I'm a bit afraid of him, boss. He's got more brains than most. I suppose, boss, that you're goin' to lay low while they're watchin' us so close, ain't you?"

"I am not," said John Flatchley, tossing away the remains of his cigarette. "Saggs, our work is almost done. One man remains—William Granner, the crookedest of the six big financial crooks. I've got to make him pay, Saggs."

"But——"

"I need about one hundred thousand dollars more, and Granner must supply it," Flatchley interrupted. "And then, Saggs, life is going to be stale for you. For I am going to stop my nefarious practices, marry, go on a honeymoon, and return and settle down. The Thunderbolt will remain one of the unsolved things on the books of the local police."

"I hope so, boss," Saggs said.

"Not afraid, are you, Saggs?"

The valet drew a long breath. "Boss, they're watchin' both of us all the time," he said. "They're watchin' this place day and night, and they watch you whenever you go out."

"Yes. And they are watching the home of my fiancée," Flatchley added. "They are watching at the club, too. But what bothers me the most is that they are guarding William Granner and his house and his office—and especially the funds that I want to get."

"Then it can't be done, boss!" Saggs declared. "You'll have to wait until they get tired of watchin'."

"I am afraid that won't do, Saggs," John Flatchley replied. "It would be a give-away."

"How's that, boss?"

"Detective Martin Radner thinks that I am The

Thunderbolt. He thinks that I have sense enough to know that I am being watched. If The Thunderbolt does not turn another trick soon, Radner will be convinced that I am The Thunderbolt and afraid to make a move because they are watching me. If I make a move and get away with it, he may be convinced that I am not the merry rogue he is so eager to catch. Understand?"

"Gosh!" Saggs breathed. "We get it goin' and we get it comin'. What are you goin' to do, boss?"

"I am going right ahead with my plans and collect from William Granner some of his ill-gotten gains," Flatchley declared without an instant of hesitation.

"With all them dicks watchin' you?"

"Exactly."

"And two or three of them sittin' on the swag you hope to cop?"

"Precisely, Saggs."

"Well, you've got a nerve!" the other declared with mingled admiration and fear in his voice. "I don't see how it can be done, boss. If you make a slip——"

"Saggs, I don't want to lead you into trouble," John Flatchley interrupted. "Far be it from me to pilot you into a mess of sorrow and remorse. And so, Saggs, you may remain quietly at home, and I'll do this last stunt by myself. If I happen to get caught, you can declare that you are merely a valet and had no idea that your employer was a crook and went around robbing people."

Saggs gulped again. "Aw, boss!" he begged. "I ain't afraid! Don't you go to pullin' off this last stunt without me havin' a hand in it, boss! You might need me bad!"

"Then that's settled," John Flatchley announced, smiling across the table at Saggs. "Come closer and lend me your ears. There are certain plans that you must know."

Saggs bent across the table, and John Flatchley talked in low whispers, now and then stopping for a moment to make sure that Saggs was understanding. When he had finished, he leaned back and lighted a fresh cigarette. Saggs gulped and looked at his employer in amazement.

"Gosh!" he breathed. "You're goin' to do it that little way, boss?"

"Exactly, Saggs."

"Of all the nerve! But she's one clever little idea, boss, at that. It'll make the local dicks look like babies. But—gee, if anything goes wrong."

Flatchley's voice was stern for a moment. "Nothing must go wrong!" he said. "You have the roadster there at the time I said, Saggs, and be careful."

"I'll be all of that, boss!"

CHAPTER XIX

HE SLIPS AWAY

AN hour later John Flatchley, resplendent in correct evening attire, went down in the elevator and stepped out to the curb, where his limousine was waiting.

He told the chauffeur to drive to the residence of Miss Agnes Larimer, and a man who happened to be passing heard the order given. Then John Flatchley got into the car and leaned back against the cushions.

The man who had heard the address given communicated it immediately to another, who promptly got into a taxicab that was waiting on the nearest corner and followed the Flatchley limousine. One of Detective Martin Radner's men was doing this shadow work, and he was determined to keep close to his quarry.

He had a lazy time of it. Flatchley got out of the limousine when the destination was reached and instructed the chauffeur to wait. The chauffeur, knowing that John Flatchley was to dine there, made himself comfortable behind the wheel and lighted a cigar. Half a block down the street the taxicab

206

stopped, and the detective who had been riding in it walked slowly along the street toward the limousine.

As he came opposite the big car he yawned, slackened his pace, and pretended to be presenting the picture of an ordinary citizen out taking the air.

"Nice evenin'," he said to the chauffeur.

"Tolerable," the chauffeur replied. He was a taciturn individual and not much given to conversation with men unknown to him.

"That's young John Flatchley's car, isn't it?" the detective asked. "Some class to that car!"

It was the only correct way to engage the chauffeur's attention.

"I should say there is some class to it!" the chauffeur declared. "When I'm driving this car, man, I'm driving the best and most expensive car in town."

"Well, John Flatchley can afford the best, I reckon," the detective observed. "He's goin' to marry Miss Larimer, I understand. She is a great girl! I've lived around this neighborhood since she was a baby--used to attend to the lawns and flowers for her aunt. She's a great girl."

"A splendid young lady, I believe," the chauffeur remarked, growing frigid again.

"Young John Flatchley is takin' dinner with the Larimers, I reckon?"

"I suppose so. However, that's his business," said the chauffeur.

"They're nice people," said the detective.

He decided that it would avail him nothing to question the chauffeur further and arouse the man's suspicions, so he strolled on to the end of the block, returned on the other side of the street, and dodged into the taxicab again when the chauffeur of the limousine was not looking in his direction.

He had a long wait of it. It was almost two hours later when John Flatchley emerged from the Larimer residence, and Agnes Larimer was with him. They got into the limousine, and Flatchley ordered the chauffeur to drive to the country club.

John Flatchley appeared to be his usual jovial self this evening. He was taking the girl he intended to make his wife to a select and private party at the club, and he knew that she easily would be the belle of the occasion.

But Agnes Larimer did not seem to be in the best of spirits. For one thing, she did not seem inclined to conversation, which puzzled Flatchley a bit.

"Tired?" he asked, after a time.

"Not tired," she replied, smiling up at him. "But I—I have been worrying a bit."

"About me?" Flatchley asked.

"Yes, John. I cannot help remembering that you have one more—adventure coming."

"My dear girl, it was our understanding that you were not to think of such things," Flatchley told her. "I cannot have you worrying, you know."

She sighed and drew closer to him. "John," she said, "I know all about it, of course, and my sympathies are with you entirely. I really think that you are doing a splendid thing in taking money from those men and giving it back to the people they swindled. But the law calls it a crime."

"Assuredly," he said.

"John, if anything should happen—if you happened to be caught in the act of——"

"I shall not be caught!" he declared. "I shall take great care in this last exploit. Do you think I'd let myself get caught when capture would mean so much for me? I'd be disgraced, I'd lose you, and you—you'd share my disgrace, in a way. Sometimes I think that I'd better stop where I am."

"You must not!" she declared. "You must go ahead with your plans. But be careful, John!"

"I'll be very careful," he answered. "This last exploit of The Thunderbolt—and then that merry rogue ceases to exist! And then, all danger over, we can be married and go away on a honeymoon without any fear of the police."

"How soon will that be?" she asked.

John Flatchley cleared his throat and seemed to be thinking for a moment. "I'd rather you did not know," he said. "Then, if an accident should happen, you can say truthfully that you knew nothing of my intentions."

"But I'd like to know, John," she said. "I'd like to be sharing your danger at least so much."

"Very well, Agnes. To-night!"

"To-night!" she gasped. "Why, we are going to the country club, and it will be at least one o'clock in the morning when we leave. It will be after two when we get home."

"And, if everything goes right, it'll all be over before we get home," Flatchley said.

"But I don't see how!"

"Dear girl, do not ask me any more," he said. "But listen to one thing—soon you are to be wholly mine, and so it would be a crime if to-night, for instance, I claimed all your time and society when so many will be wanting to dance with you. And if you should not see me for an hour or so, you might mention that I am letting the other fellows have their last chance—that I'm somewhere about, possibly playing billiards."

"Oh!" she gasped. "You are going to do it while the party is in progress? But how?"

"Little girls should not know too much," Flatchley replied, laughing. "I do not want you to worry."

As the limousine turned into the long, tree-bordered driveway that led to the entrance of the club, John Flatchley was smiling. When the big car came to a stop, he assisted Agnes Larimer to alight, and friends rushed forward to greet them.

Then the chauffeur drove to the rear of the club building, where parking space was provided, and after putting the limousine in its proper place he repaired to the little building set apart for the use of waiting chauffeurs, there to talk with others of his kind.

The pursuing taxicab did not enter the club grounds. But the detective who was its passenger did. He made his way carefully through the darkness, keeping away from the lights on the drive, and approached the parking space.

He located John Flatchley's big car immediately, and heard the Flatchley chauffeur talking to another. Dropping down behind a clump of valuable shrubs, the detective made himself as comfortable as possible.

He had his eyes on the Flatchley limousine, and he could watch the front entrance of the club, and he judged that was all that was necessary. When the party was at an end, and John Flatchley got into the limousine again, then the detective would once more take up his task of shadowing.

Inside the club John Flatchley spent the first half hour as is customary at such affairs. He greeted his friends and acquaintances, made himself popular anew with the ladies, had a first dance with Agnes Larimer, and then wandered through a hall and toward the billiard room.

He refused to handle a cue, however, though

urged to do so. He made the rounds of the club, dropping into the lounging room for a moment and listening to an argument about golf, into the smoking room to watch a card game for high stakes played by some of the city's financiers. Almost everybody there saw John Flatchley during that first half hour. He registered on their minds the fact that he was present, and, if anybody happened to ask for him later, that person would be told that he was "around somewhere."

The crowd was large, and the club building was jammed, and for these things John Flatchley was grateful. It made the consummation of his plans much easier. He gradually got away from his near friends and went toward the rear of the building.

Finally he slipped through a side door and made his way to the dark end of a veranda. He waited there for a moment, as though admiring the fine summer night, and then, sure that he was not being observed, he sprang over the railing and to the ground.

There he paused in the darkness for a moment, and then he darted swiftly and silently toward a deeper shadow cast by a big maple tree. Crouching there for a time he listened to the loud talk of the waiting chauffeurs in their rest room, watched the couples on the front veranda, assured himself that there was nobody taking an interest in his movements.

Then he went from shadow to shadow, until he reached the edge of a grove in the rear of the club buildings. He hurried through the grove, keeping a short distance from the paths, and came to the fence that divided the club grounds from other property.

Vaulting the fence, John Flatchley crossed the dusty road and plunged into the woods beyond. A hundred yards he traveled, and then he emerged into another road. Standing back in the darkness, John Flatchley gave a peculiar whistle.

It was answered immediately. Along the road, lights extinguished, came a powerful roadster. It stopped when Flatchley signaled, and he sprang toward it. The voice of Saggs reached his ears.

"All right, boss! Here we are! Have any trouble makin' a get-away?"

"Not a bit, Saggs. How about yourself?"

"Ain't got any complaints," Saggs declared. "Wasn't a hard job at all."

John Flatchley had reached the side of the car. He took off his evening coat, folded it carefully, and handed it to Saggs to put into a pocket. He took from Saggs' hands an ordinary black coat, and put it on and turned up the collar and buttoned it. He slipped on a pair of thin, black trousers that covered his evening things and belted them around his waist beneath the coat.

He sat down on the running board of the car, removed his pumps, handed them to Saggs to put away, and pulled on a pair of heavy shoes that looked two sizes larger than the pumps. Then he put on a dark cap and pulled it down low over his eyes.

"All right, Saggs!" he said, springing into the car. "You can do the driving, and remember your instructions. You didn't forget that Thunderbolt stuff, did you?"

"It's in the secret pocket, boss."

"Good enough! Let's go!"

Flatchley sank back into the seat. Saggs drove slowly until he reached the main highway, and then he turned on the lights and went toward the city at a high rate of speed.

CHAPTER XX

ON THE JOB

SAGGS had waited for an hour after the departure of John Flatchley from the suite; then he had gone to the front window and looked down at the street. As he had expected, he saw a detective standing opposite on guard.

He went back into the kitchen, lifted a window there, and peered down into the alley. A man he knew to be another detective was loitering there, talking to a janitor from the apartment house next door.

Saggs grinned and then muttered things about detectives in general. He hurried back to the living room, placed a chair before the front window, and sat in it, noticing that his shadow was on the shade. He knew that the detective across the street could see the shadow.

For about fifteen minutes Saggs sat there, to give the impression to the watcher that he was reading. He left the chair for a time, then, and presently returned with a roll of bedding around one end of which he had fastened a necktie. Careful not to throw a shadow, he approached the chair and managed to brace the roll of bedding in it properly. He glanced at the shade. The shadow was that of a man sitting in a chair, reading.

Saggs stepped back and chuckled. He snapped out one of the lights, so that the shadow was not so distinct. And then he got his cap, put it on, let himself into the corridor from the tiny kitchen, and walked briskly toward the rear of the building.

But he did not descend the rear stairs to the alley entrance. He wished to avoid the man on guard there. Instead, he ascended to the top floor of the building, went to a side window, opened it, and got out on the roof of the building adjoining.

Slipping noiselessly across this roof, he came to a fire escape that ran down into a little court that was in darkness. Saggs went down the fire escape like a monkey, reached the pavement below, watched for a time, and slipped into the alley proper.

Keeping to the dark spaces, he came to the cross street, turned into it, and hurried a block to the garage where John Flatchley kept his cars. Before entering the garage he made certain that there was nobody there except the regular two night attendants and a third man washing cars in the rear.

Saggs entered boldly, as he had done hundreds of times.

"Roll out the old roadster," he told the night man in charge.

"Goin' to take a little spin while the boss is out

with the limousine, are you?" the attendant asked, grinning.

"Don't you care!" Saggs grunted.

"I don't boy. Go as far as you like. The tank's full of gas, and she's got oil and water."

"Matter-of-fact," said Saggs, "Mr. Flatchley wanted me to take her out to the speedway and limber her up a bit. He hasn't used the roadster for some time, and he thought she acted a bit sluggish the last time."

"If she does it again, let us know, and we'll put pep into her," said the attendant.

Saggs drove from the garage, went slowly through the streets, came to the speedway, increased his speed, and finally took the road toward the country club. He glanced at his watch once, and found that he would be on time.

As he approached the club he took a road that ran behind it, and after a time, sure that there was nobody else near, he snapped off the lights, throttled down to a crawl, left the main road, and followed a rough, rutty thoroughfare that ran back into the woods, a highway used by farmers getting out wood for the winter.

Saggs watched carefully until he came to a certain tree that John Flatchley had mentioned. Then he turned the powerful roadster around, backed it out of the road and into the brush, and waited. While he waited he made sure that the tires were in perfect condition, that the car was ready for a hot run if one proved to be necessary.

In time John Flatchley came to him through the woods, and they began their drive to the city.

"You'd better be careful to-night, boss!" Saggs warned. "If anything happens——"

"Pessimistic again, are you, Saggs? You'll be glad, I suppose, when this last stunt of ours is over."

"I'll feel a bit easier, boss," the other admitted. "It's a tough game, with all the cops in town watchin' you. Suppose they missed you at the club? Suppose——"

"You can suppose a thousand things if you make up your mind to do it," The Thunderbolt told him. "Suppose, for instance, that everything goes off smoothly. That's the best way."

"All right, boss," murmured the valet.

"Take the back streets, Saggs. I don't want to be recognized, you know, and I don't care to put on The Thunderbolt's hood until I reach my destination."

The Thunderbolt said nothing more after that. Saggs piloted the big car through streets that had little traffic, and whenever he was forced to pass another vehicle he put on speed and passed it as quickly as possible.

They reached the wholesale district and went block after block over the smooth pavements, until they came to the retail district and the section of tall office buildings.

Saggs began to use more caution then. He slowed down the car, and he conversed with The Thunderbolt in low tones. And after a time he stopped the roadster just at the mouth of an alley, got out and lifted the hood, and pretended to be investigating the engine.

The Thunderbolt reached back and touched a button that opened a secret pocket. From this pocket he took a thin pair of black gloves, the hood worn by The Thunderbolt, an automatic, and an electric torch, all rolled into a compact bundle.

He glanced up and down the street and through the alley, made sure that nobody was in sight, and then slipped quickly from the car and into the dark space before the building. There he waited for an instant, gave Saggs his last instructions, and darted into the alley.

The valet closed the hood of the machine, got behind the wheel, and traveled on. He knew better than to keep the car near the place where The Thunderbolt intended to work. At a certain time he would return, and until that time he would travel through the downtown district, like a man out motoring for the pure joy of it.

The Thunderbolt crept carefully through the alley until he came to the rear of a huge office building, on the third floor of which William Granner had his suite of offices. He glanced up and saw that the lights were burning in the Granner suite, which was what he had expected to find.

He knew the building well, for his own attorney had offices there, also on the third floor. Two weeks before, The Thunderbolt, during a visit had made a wax impression of certain keys, and afterward had other keys made from the impressions, but in such a way that the work could not be traced to him. He even had tried out the keys on a subsequent visit to his attorney.

He slipped into a dark, narrow space between two buildings, watched and listened for a time, and then took from the pocket of his coat a length of fine, strong rope. It was scarcely larger than a fishing cord, but it had the strength of a hawser.

Putting the rope to one side, The Thunderbolt donned his hood and gloves, and stowed away his automatic and electric torch. He stepped back, tossed up one end of the fine rope, which had been weighted, and looped it through the lower part of the fire escape above.

The weight came down to him, and The Thunderbolt grasped both strands of the rope, braced his feet against the side of the building, and started climbing noiselessly. He came to the first landing of the fire escape and stopped to rest, drawing up the rope and leaving it coiled there.

The fire escape was in darkness as far up as the

fourth floor, for the adjoining building cut off the light from the distant street. The Thunderbolt hesitated no longer. He went up the steel ladder until he reached the window at the third floor, and there he stepped back against the building to watch and listen again. Fifty feet to one side, lights were shining in the offices of William Granner.

From his coat lining The Thunderbolt took an ordinary burglar's jimmy. He used it on the window and snapped the light-weight catch. An instant later he was inside the building and had closed the window carefully after him.

Now he slipped to the main hall and glanced up and down. There was a watchman on this floor of the building, but he was not in sight. The Thunderbolt darted to the door that opened into the suite of offices occupied by his lawyer, used the key he had obtained, and let himself in.

Locking the door behind him, he went into the private office, and through that to a room used for files of documents, where the attorney's clerks worked. Just on the other side of that room was the first room of William Granner's suite.

The Thunderbolt knelt beside the door and peered through the keyhole. The next room was in darkness, but the room beyond was well lighted. The door between the rooms was open. The Thunderbolt, looking through and into the second room, could see two members of the city's detective force sitting at a table, playing cards, smoking, talking.

He fitted a key in the lock and turned it carefully. He did not succeed in unlocking the door at first, but after a time it yielded. And then he knelt and peered through the keyhole again. The two men in the second room had not moved from their positions. They were still playing cards.

The Thunderbolt noticed that the streak of light which came from that second room did not illuminate the space in front of the door behind which he crouched. Yet opening that door would be a hazard. If one of the men happened to glance up, he would be seen. And he did not want that. He wished to catch them off guard and get them at a disadvantage.

He knew the two detectives. From one of them he had nothing to fear, but the other was a man almost as good as Detective Martin Radner, a man who might be expected to take a chance in an effort to outwit such a man as The Thunderbolt.

The Thunderbolt opened the door an inch, glad to find that the hinges made no noise. He waited an instant, then opened it wider and looked inside the room. The two men were finishing a game and were excited. They were laughing and talking loudly. The Thunderbolt slipped through and closed the door behind him. Silently he darted to one side and crouched behind a desk.

In William Granner's inner office the two detectives had started a new deal. The Thunderbolt could hear their conversation easily.

"Mighty slow around here," one of them was saying. "If you ask me, The Thunderbolt won't make a show while we're on the job. He's no fool! He'll wait until Radner gets tired and stops watching so closely, and then he'll break out in some new place. And while we're watching Granner's office, The Thunderbolt probably will tackle somebody else."

"Just as soon be here taking it easy as out on some tough job," the other remarked. "As far as The Thunderbolt is concerned——"

He happened to glance through the door. His lower jaw sagged, his eyes bulged, and he dropped his cards and slowly lifted his hands. The man across the table glanced up and saw this, and whirled to look at the door.

The Thunderbolt stood there, covering them with an automatic pistol. His eyes glittered ominously through the slits in the hood he wore. He spoke in a hoarse monotone:

"Not a move, gentlemen! Don't try to touch that bell button! A slight motion might make my trigger finger nervous, you know! Up with your hands!"

The Thunderbolt was watching both of them, but

particularly the man he knew to be the more daring of the two.

"You——" the detective began.

"And not a word, please!" The Thunderbolt instructed. "Do as I say, and we'll get along nicely together. Try a trick, and you'll probably be in the morgue in an hour or so. Think it over!"

The Thunderbolt stepped farther into the room, stepped closer to them, menacing them with the automatic. His left hand dived into a pocket of his coat, and he drew out another coil of the small, strong rope. He tossed it on the table, and beckoned to the man of whom he was not afraid.

"Stand up, come to me, and turn your back!" The Thunderbolt commanded.

The man obeyed, for he did not see the sense of courting instant death by refusing. Just because The Thunderbolt never had shot a man was no reason for believing that he would not do so if the occasion demanded it.

Still holding his hands above his head, he stepped forward and turned his back. The Thunderbolt, watching the other man closely, reached forward and got revolver and handcuffs from the one who stood in front of him. He slipped the revolver into his pocket; he tossed the handcuffs on the table.

"Now go back to the table, take those handcuffs, and put them on your friend!" The Thunderbolt ordered.

"Kelly, if you do——" the man at the table began.

"Oh, do not blame Kelly, if that is his name," said The Thunderbolt. "What else can he do? Hurry about it, Kelly. I'm getting nervous!"

Detective Kelly gasped, but went to the table and picked up the handcuffs. He knew that he should attempt to do something to disconcert The Thunderbolt, but what could he do without a weapon? And the man at the table did not seem to want to make a move and attempt to shoot it out.

"Hurry!" The Thunderbolt commanded. "And see that you handcuff him good, too! I don't want any careless work, you understand!"

Kelly walked around the table, the handcuffs held ready. The two detectives were watching The Thunderbolt as closely as he was watching them. They failed to catch him off guard even for an instant.

The Thunderbolt took another step forward, and his eyes glittered as he stooped over the end of the table.

"Hurry!" he commanded again.

There was a sharp click, and the man at the table was ironed.

The Thunderbolt waved Detective Kelly back against the wall. He darted forward and searched the handcuffed man, took away another revolver and another pair of handcuffs. He stepped back and motioned Detective Kelly again.

"Take that cord on the table and bind his arms and legs!" he ordered. "And see that you do a good job of it, Kelly, if you want to continue drawing pay from the city. Don't pay any attention to him if he raves a bit. You can't help what you're doing, you know."

"I'll get you for this if it takes ten years!" the man at the table muttered angrily.

"It is your privilege to try," The Thunderbolt told him. "Join forces with Radner and go to it! I like to deal with worthy foes."

"I'll get you——"

"Possibly. But let us attend to business now," The Thunderbolt said. "Lie on the floor, and let Kelly bind you. Do it—or I'll stretch you there with a smash on the head!"

There was a stern ring to The Thunderbolt's voice. Cursing audibly, the detective got up and stepped back from the table. He glanced quickly around the room like a cornered beast.

"Do not try it!" The Thunderbolt warned. "You attempt to send an alarm in any way, and it'll be your last attempt! Lie down on the floor!"

The detective wished now that he had whipped out his revolver at first and made an attempt to get The Thunderbolt. But it was too late. He had no weapon, he was handcuffed, and if he tried to make a move The Thunderbolt probably would shoot him down and make his get-away.

He cursed The Thunderbolt, and he cursed himself, but he stretched out on the floor, and Detective Kelly, with The Thunderbolt's eyes upon him, quickly bound his comrade. When he had finished he stepped back, and The Thunderbolt went forward and examined the bonds.

"A fair job!" he commented. "Sorry to handle you gentlemen like this, but I can't be having you interfere with my business, you know. And you have one consolation—you're not the only ones. I've handled Detective Martin Radner before now."

He took another small coil of rope from his pocket, and once more he beckoned Detective Kelly.

"On the floor," he ordered. "I'll bind you myself."

Kelly did not hesitate. Stretched on the floor, he made no resistance while The Thunderbolt fastened his ankles and wrists. Then The Thunderbolt lashed the two detectives together, afterward tying them in turn to a radiator in one corner of the office.

"Now you won't be able to roll around the office and give an alarm and bother me," The Thunderbolt said. "Now for the gags!"

"You dare to gag us——" the belligerent detective began.

"Tut, tut!" said The Thunderbolt. "Certainly I

shall gag you. Can't be having you make a noise, you know. If you did that, I'd have to shoot, and I don't want to if it can be avoided."

They struggled a little, but The Thunderbolt soon had them gagged effectually. Those coat pockets of his seemed to contain everything he needed. When he had finished he stepped back and looked them over, and they heard him chuckling behind his hood.

"Now you will keep out of mischief!" he told them. "Also, you can watch this affair and tell a good story about it afterward. It'll be interesting, I assure you. And now—the telephone!"

CHAPTER XXI

CAUGHT IN A TRAP

WILLIAM GRANNER sat before his desk in his library and read the financial pages of the evening newspapers. In another corner of the room two members of the city's detective force sprawled on a large divan, also reading. Granner knew that a third man paraded around the house, keeping a close watch.

Glancing at the clock on the desk before him, Granner saw that it was a couple of minutes after the hour of ten. He yawned and stretched his arms and thought of bed, for he had an important business conference the following day, and he wanted to be fresh for it.

"Guess I'll turn in!" he announced. "If you men want anything, just ring for it. One of the servants will stay up to attend to you. There'll be a lunch served at midnight."

"Much obliged, sir," one of the officers replied. "It does get monotonous, sitting around and doing nothing. But we both like to read and we can play cards."

"Don't forget to keep awake," Granner said,

smiling. "We don't want The Thunderbolt to slip in here and get at my safe."

"I don't think he'll try it, Mr. Granner. He'll probably stay off the job as long as your place is being guarded. And the chances are that he is more interested in your office than your residence. However, if he does show up around here, we'll try to take care of him. Good night, sir."

Granner got up and started toward the hall door. The telephone bell jingled.

Stepping back to his desk, the financier took up the instrument and put the receiver to his ear.

"Hello!" he called.

"Is this Mr. Granner?"

"Yes."

"Please come to your office at once, Mr. Granner. This is Detective Kelly speaking."

"But what——"

William Granner heard a soft click and knew that the receiver had been hung up at the other end of the line. He turned toward the officers.

"Call from the office," he said, his face suddenly ashen. "Said he was Detective Kelly and wants me to come down at once."

The detectives got to their feet.

"Maybe it is The Thunderbolt, sir," one of them said. "Maybe they have caught him. You are going?"

"At once!" Granner replied. He touched a button

to notify his chauffeur to bring a car to the front of the house immediately.

"I'll just ring that call back," one of the officers said.

He hurried to the telephone, asked Granner the number of his office, and put in the call. Central answered that the line was busy.

"Bet a dollar they've caught The Thunderbolt, and Kelly is giving the news to the papers!" the detective said. "Hard luck for us! Kelly and his pal will get all the glory."

"I'll hurry right down——" Granner began. He was nervous and showed symptoms of fear. "One of you men going with me?"

"We'd better not, sir," one of them replied. "It may be a trick, you know, to get us away from the house. Go with your chauffeur, sir—that is, unless you are afraid to——"

"I am not afraid!" Granner replied in a stern voice, and the two detectives had hard work to conceal their smiles, for they knew fear when they saw it.

He hurried into the hall, got his hat, and rushed to the front of the house. The chauffeur drove around in a closed car, and William Granner sprang in and gave his destination. The car rolled away.

"Maybe it's all right, and maybe it isn't," one of the detectives told the other. "It won't do any hurt to telephone headquarters and try to get Radner, I guess."

He sat down before the telephone, and this time he got his call through immediately. He asked for Detective Radner and waited.

Radner was at headquarters, but it took some minutes to find him. When he answered the telephone, the detective at the. Granner house gave him the information in a few words:

"Granner just got a telephone message for him to hurry down to his office, and he's gone. He said Kelly telephoned. Anything doing? I thought I'd better let you know."

"Haven't heard a word from the office," Radner replied. "Glad you phoned: I'll investigate."

The detective at the house went back to his book. He had done all that the occasion demanded.

William Granner sat on the edge of the seat as his car carried him through the streets of the residence section and quickly into the business district. He felt fear, though he did not know why he should. If The Thunderbolt had raided his offices, then Granner told himself what he would do to certain members of the local police department.

When the car stopped before the entrance to the building, Granner glanced up and saw the lights burning in his suite. He hurried to the elevator, and the night man clanged the door shut and reached for the lever.

"Anything—er—unusual been happening?" Granner asked.

"No, sir. It's been a quiet night, Mr. Granner."

"Nice weather," Granner observed lamely.

He did not know what else to say. He got out of the elevator and hurried along the corridor to the front door of his own suite. The door was unlocked, and Granner opened it quickly and stepped inside. There was nobody in the front office. The door to the private office was open, and the lights were burning there, but no sound came from the room.

With his heart hammering at his ribs William Granner stepped quickly and as silently as possible across the room to the door of the inner office. As he did so, a shadow came from behind a row of file cases and followed the financier.

Granner did not know what he expected to find. As he neared the door he seemed to hear a groan, and it sent shivers up and down his spine. He came to the door, bent forward and peered inside, and gulped with greater fear.

He saw the two officers, bound and gagged, stretched on the floor and lashed to the radiator. He glanced quickly around the office, but saw nothing else to cause him alarm. The big door of the vault was closed. Nothing seemed to have been disturbed.

Another groan from one of the detectives seemed to bring William Granner to a realization of the officers' predicament. He stepped inside the office and started across toward them. A voice behind him caused him to stop.

"One moment, Mr. Granner!" it said.

Even as he whirled around William Granner admitted to himself that there was something ominous about that hoarse voice. He turned—and looked into the muzzle of an automatic. He saw The Thunderbolt before him, saw the black hood with its devilish device, the eyes glittering through the slits in it.

William Granner almost collapsed. It flashed through his mind that he was at The Thunderbolt's mercy, that The Thunderbolt had rendered the two detectives helpless.

"Do not be unduly alarmed, Mr. Granner," The Thunderbolt said. "No harm will come to you if you are kind enough to do as I say, and without hesitation. Otherwise, I am afraid that I shall have to deal harshly with you."

"You——you" Granner tried to speak.

"Paralysis of the vocal cords?" The Thunderbolt asked pleasantly. "Possibly the less you speak the better. Your faithful guardians of the office funds are unable to aid you, you will notice. I am glad that you answered my telephone message and came alone. I was ready, in fact, to handle those who might come with you. But matters are simplified now. I shall detain you but a few minutes—I hope."

"What—do you want?" Granner managed to ask.

"That's better! Now we can get down to business!" The Thunderbolt told him.

He stepped a pace nearer, and William Granner recoiled.

"I want you to open that vault—and at once!" The Thunderbolt said. "Make just one false move, and this city will have one financier less! Be quick!"

"But——" Granner began.

"Want to argue with me?" The Thunderbolt cut in. "Tired of living and squeezing money out of people, are you? You can replace any funds I happen to take, you know, but if I am forced to shoot you, you'll have a hard time replacing your living self. Are you going to open that vault?"

"Yes—yes! I'll open it!"

"And be quick about it, Granner! It makes me nervous to wait, and when I get nervous my trigger finger has a habit of contracting. So consider yourself warned!"

William Granner staggered toward the vault and knelt before the heavy door. He fumbled at the combination knob. He was not a very courageous man at best, and in this emergency he was terribly frightened.

He glanced helplessly at the two bound and gagged detectives. He mourned the financial loss he was afraid he was about to sustain. For he had ample funds in the vault—Liberty Bonds he had been purchasing, other negotiable bonds, currency, valuable papers the loss of which would cause him trouble and annoyance.

He worked the combination, got to his feet, and pulled the heavy door open. The Thunderbolt had reached beneath his coat and taken out a sack made of very thin material. He unfolded it and stepped forward.

"Go into the vault ahead of me and turn on the light!" he commanded.

William Granner did not hesitate. He stepped inside, snapped on the light, and found that The Thunderbolt was standing just behind him. There was a revolver in that vault, within five feet of where Granner was standing, but he had no thought of attempting to get it and firing at The Thunderbolt. Something seemed to tell him that such a move would be the same as suicide.

"What do you want now?" Granner gasped.

"I want Liberty Bonds—the bigger the better," The Thunderbolt replied. "And I want coupon bonds. Make no mistake about that. I have no use for the registered variety. You have plenty of them—you've been buying them at a discount from people who needed money, you crook! Get them for me—coupon bonds only—and we'll fill the sack!"

"But——"

"And spare me your talk!" The Thunderbolt ordered. "All I want from you is action—quick action at that! I'm commencing to grow nervous again!"

William Granner groaned and opened a compartment in the vault. He sat down on a little stool before it and began taking out bundles of bonds. He tossed the registered bonds aside and put the coupon bonds in the sack The Thunderbolt was holding. Each time he dumped in a bundle he looked at the automatic, and found that, though The Thunderbolt was holding the sack with both hands, he still held the automatic in his right hand also, and kept it pointed at the financier.

"That's all the coupon bonds," Granner muttered after a time.

"How much?" The Thunderbolt asked.

"A hundred thousand—possibly a bit more. This will ruin me!"

"Don't be a baby!" The Thunderbolt exclaimed. "It'll only make a dent in your bank roll. You'll keep right on putting across shady financial deals and making your huge profits. You whine once more, Granner, and I'll strip your vault clean! But this is enough for to-night. It is all that I need at present. Follow me out of the vault, now!"

The financier obeyed gladly, for he had been afraid that The Thunderbolt might lock him in the vault and leave him to suffocate. At The Thunderbolt's command he closed the heavy door and whirled the combination knob. And then he collapsed in the nearest chair, holding his shaking hands to his face.

"You are a fine specimen of a man!" The Thunderbolt said sneeringly. "You're brave enough when you're manipulating the market and fleecing lambs, but not much good in a personal clash. A boy could handle you, Granner! I'm ashamed of the fact that I held a gun on you! You're not worth so much attention."

"What are you going to do with me now?" William Granner asked querulously.

"Tie you up and make my get-away," The Thunderbolt replied.

He took another short length of that small, strong rope from one of his coat pockets and advanced upon the terrified William Granner.

"Stretch out on the floor, flat on your stomach, and put your hands behind your back!" The Thunderbolt commanded. "And be quick about it, if you want me to be merciful. I can be violent just as easy, you understand!"

The financier did not voice a protest. He did not have courage enough to utter a word. He dropped to the floor and stretched out upon it, and almost instantly The Thunderbolt had his wrists lashed behind his back. He lashed Granner's ankles together, too, and then rolled him over beside the two helpless and glaring detectives.

"Now a little gag, Mr. Granner, and I am done," The Thunderbolt declared. He affixed the gag despite Granner's half-hysterical mouthings. "And now I'd advise you to calm yourself, unless you are eager to bring on a stroke of apoplexy. Do not worry, Granner. I'll telephone Detective Martin Radner to come to the office at once and release you."

A voice came from the door:

"It isn't necessary to waste time telephoning!"

The Thunderbolt sprang to his feet and whirled around. Detective Martin Radner stood in the doorway, bending forward slightly, a wicked-looking police revolver held ready for business!

CHAPTER XXII

FROM A TRASH CAN

E ASY!" Detective Martin Radner warned, his eyes glittering as he watched The Thunderbolt narrowly. "Toss that automatic over in the corner! Be quick about it!"

The Thunderbolt seemed to hesitate for an instant, seemed to be estimating his chances if he offered a show of resistance. Detective Radner's revolver was elevated a couples of inches more, until the muzzle of it was directed straight at The Thunderbolt's breast and the officer's voice had a ring of determination in it when he spoke again.

"Don't try any tricks!" Radner advised. "You'll be a dead man if you make a move! Better be sensible about it. Toss that gun to the corner!"

In that instant The Thunderbolt became John Flatchley for a moment. For the second time in his career as The Thunderbolt, he had a vision of trial and sentence, utter disgrace, the consternation of his friends and acquaintances, sensational headlines in the newspapers. He saw Agnes Larimer with her head bowed in sorrow, saw his future life ruined.

But it was only for an instant. The moment of

240

panic passed, and he became The Thunderbolt again, cold, calculating, thinking ahead, his brain alert. From behind the hood came the sound of a sigh— and he tossed the automatic to the corner of the room as Detective Radner had ordered.

"So!" Radner said. "We have you at last, have we? I'll say one thing for you—you certainly did lead us a merry chase. You are clever, all right— if my compliment will do you any good. But you made one little mistake to-night. The men at the Granner residence telephoned me about your message to Mr. Granner, and I hurried down here to make a little investigation. It didn't sound good to me. However, none of us is perfect."

"I suppose not," The Thunderbolt replied in a hoarse voice that expressed resignation to fate.

Detective Martin Radner took another step forward. "I am rather anxious to have a look at that face of yours," he said. "I have been speculating a great deal about your identity. I've been thinking one thing, and the chief has been thinking another. We'll know soon which of us is right. Or possibly we are both wrong."

"Possibly," The Thunderbolt replied.

He had not made a move since tossing the automatic away. He stood with his back against the wall, his hands at his sides, his head held high.

"Suppose you unbind one of my men now," Detective Radner directed. "Then he can unbind the others, and we can get down to business."

"You scarcely can expect me to do your work for you," The Thunderbolt said, with some hostility in his manner. "Isn't it enough that you've got me? And I scarcely think that you'll shoot me down if I refuse. So perhaps you'd better do your own work —you're paid for it."

"Think you'll make some sort of a break while I'm doing it, do you?" Detective Radner said sneeringly. "You just try it, my man! I've been on your trail entirely too long to have you play a trick on me now. You've already played a few, remember, and I've yet to square accounts with you for those."

"You've squared them by catching me, haven't you?" The Thunderbolt asked.

"You stand over in that other corner and hold your arms high above your head!"

"Oh, I'll do that!" replied The Thunderbolt. "You have a right to command that—but I'll not untie those prisoners."

He moved slowly to the corner Detective Radner had indicated, and stood there with his back against the wall, his arms stretched up above his head. The detective felt for his handcuffs, but discovering he had forgotten them, he went toward Kelly. As he knelt to unfasten the handcuffs from Kelly, Radner watched The Thunderbolt closely.

Through the slits in the front of the hood he wore The Thunderbolt watched carefully. He saw that Radner was about to remove the handcuffs from Detective Kelly. And Kelly, as soon as he was unbound, would tell what The Thunderbolt did not want Detective Radner to know—that in his coat pocket The Thunderbolt had the revolver he had taken from him.

Detective Martin Radner fumbled at the handcuffs, but their mechanism seemed to have become jammed. And then he did what The Thunderbolt had been hoping he would do—he turned his eyes just for an instant to locate the difficulty.

In that same instant The Thunderbolt moved. He darted to one side. His hand dived into the pocket of his coat and came out holding Detective Kelly's revolver. Even as Radner turned and fired, the shot smashing into the wall where The Thunderbolt had been standing, The Thunderbolt fired twice, and the two gleaming incandescent globes over the big table in the middle of the room were shattered to fragments, and the room plunged in darkness.

Radner fired again. The Thunderbolt darted through the door to the outer office, pressed the light switch, and plunged that room in darkness also. He darted to the corridor door, opened it and ran through as another bullet from Detective Radner's revolver whistled past his head. He slammed the door after him. That gave him a moment.

A single glance showed him that fortunately the watchman was not in the corridor. He heard one of them yelling on the floor above, though. He ran to the door of his lawyer's suite, let himself in as he had earlier in the night, darted through to the door that communicated with the Granner offices, and crouched there, trying to see through the keyhole.

Detective Radner had run out into the corridor. There he met the watchman from the floor above. He whistled, and other watchmen in the building came running. The first snapped on the lights in the outer office of the Granner suite, took out one of the globes, and hurried to the inner office and put it into a socket there. The inner office was illuminated.

The Thunderbolt locked the door behind which he was crouching, and watched and listened. The watchman was unfastening the two detectives and William Granner. The detectives charged through the outer office and to the corridor to back up the efforts of Detective Martin Radner. The Thunderbolt could hear them calling at one another in the halls, on the floor above and below. Somebody was frantically ringing the elevator bell.

William Granner, his face white, tottered to the door of the outer office and leaned against the casement, holding one hand to his head. Looking past him, The Thunderbolt could see the sack of bonds on the end of the table. He did not intend to leave without those bonds, but he would run a great risk getting them.

He guessed that Radner was calling more officers, that the block would be swarming with them soon, that a careful search would be made of the entire building and the buildings adjoining. Radner would not quit easily when once he had had The Thunderbolt at his mercy.

Nor could he afford to linger long in the attorney's office. Saggs would be waiting at a certain corner with the roadster. Time was flying. The Thunderbolt would have to return to the country club and become John Flatchley again.

He reached forward and unlocked the door once more. He glanced through the keyhole and saw that Granner was standing some distance in front of the door to the inner office, looking out at the corridor.

Opening the door softly, The Thunderbolt suddenly sprang into the room. Granner whirled and saw him, and uttered a cry of fear.

"Silence!" Thunderbolt commanded. He did not have any fear of William Granner, but he did of the officers scattered through the building. He hurled the financier to one side, darted into the inner office, seized the sack of bonds, ran back, hurled Granner to one side again, and darted into the attorney's office once more, stopping to lock the door behind him.

Granner's shrieks now rang through the building. Some of the officers came charging back. The Thunderbolt ran quickly to the corridor door, unlocked it, and glanced out. He saw Kelly and another man just running into Granner's office.

He did not hesitate now. Out into the corridor he ran, to the little cross hall, to the window by which he had entered the building. He raised it and got through, slithered rapidly down the fire escape and dropped the rope he had left coiled on the first landing. Down it he went as speedily as possible until his feet touched the ground. There he crouched in the darkness for a moment, panting, listening, watching.

He could hear cries in the building he had just left. Lights were flashing on the other floors. From the street in front came the shrieking of a siren, and The Thunderbolt knew that additional men were arriving from police headquarters.

The Thunderbolt made the sack of bonds as compact as possible and slipped it beneath his coat. He removed his hood and stowed it away, also the thin black gloves. He was glad of one thing—the automatic he had left behind could not be traced to him, and there were no finger prints on it.

He crept to the alley, put out his head, glanced up and down. Nobody was in sight, but he could not be sure that an officer was not lurking in the darkness. But he started toward the distant street, keeping in the shadows, scarcely making a sound.

On he went, stopping now and then to watch and listen. He tugged at his cap and pulled it down more over his eyes. He did not care to have anybody say that they had seen John Flatchley in the neighborhood.

He was almost at the mouth of the alley now. Into it from the street came two patrolmen. The Thunderbolt crouched against the rear wall of a building in the darkness. They came toward him, talking to each other, flashing their electric torches.

The Thunderbolt feared those torch flashes. If one happened to fall upon him, and he was discovered, he would face a crisis. He clutched Detective Kelly's revolver again, bent lower against the building's wall.

What he had feared happened. One of the officers flashed his torch, and the light struck against The Thunderbolt. The patrolmen stopped.

"Come out of that——"

The Thunderbolt came! He sprang aside and forward. One shot he fired from the revolver, firing high purposely, more to disconcert the men before him than to injure. He had no wish to wound an officer performing his duty. He had avoided that so far.

Down the alley he ran, darting from side to side in the darkness, bending forward. Behind him, two revolvers cracked, and the bullets whistled past uncomfortably near.

Now he was at the mouth of the alley. He met another patrolman running into the alley, crashed against him, and floored him. He darted into the street and ran with the speed of the wind toward the avenue half a block beyond.

Three cursing, angry pursuers were behind him now. But The Thunderbolt, more than he feared them, was afraid that others would be attracted by the tumult, that he would run into new arrivals on the scene and find himself cornered.

But he reached the avenue in safety and glanced wildly up and down. Saggs and the roadster were not in sight. He had instructed Saggs to drive slowly around a couple of blocks after a certain time, saying that he would dart out and spring into the machine from some hiding place. Saggs, he supposed, had the roadster on some other street at the moment.

His pursuers would be at the corner in a moment. There were doorways handy, but none would be safe. At the curb was a big trash can. The Thunderbolt could do nothing but trust to that.

The big, galvanized receptacle had been emptied by the street-cleaning department less than half an hour before, and there was nothing in it. The Thunderbolt got in and doubled himself until his head was below the level.

He heard the officers as they rounded the corner, heard their feet pounding on the walk. They stopped within fifteen feet of the trash can, and The Thunderbolt could hear them talking, knew that they were searching the doorways.

"He's made it to the next corner," said a gruff voice. "The way he was going he's halfway across town by now."

They hurried on down the street toward the next corner. The Thunderbolt waited until the sounds they made died away in the distance, and then he raised his head cautiously until he could look over the edge of the trash can.

Not a policeman was in sight. A block down the street, a belated pedestrian was hurrying along the walk, his back toward The Thunderbolt. And coming up the street was The Thunderbolt's powerful roadster, loafing along, Saggs behind the wheel.

Mr. Saggs was somewhat shocked and surprised to see a trash can roll off the curb. But he was moved to action when he saw The Thunderbolt spring out of it and dart to the car and jump in.

"Drive!" The Thunderbolt ordered.

Mr. Saggs drove, and he forgot the traffic regulations when he did so.

The big roadster roared through the retail district, the wholesale district, and out upon the country road that led toward the country club. Then Saggs spoke.

"Did you get away with it, boss?" he asked.

"Why, Saggs, you surprise me," The Thunderbolt declared. "Don't I always get away with it?"

Now they were running along the highway close to the river, and the road was in darkness. The Thunderbolt removed the sack of bonds from beneath his coat. They were approaching the place where the road forked.

"Slow down!" The Thunderbolt commanded. "You remember the rest of your instructions, Saggs?"

"Sure do, boss."

"Keep on going after I leave the car. Swing around the club and go back to the city by the other road. Then put up the car and get back into the suite."

"I gotcha, boss."

The Thunderbolt was taking off the big shoes he wore and putting on his pumps again. He took his dress coat out of the secret pocket. The roadster was slowed down, and The Thunderbolt sprang lightly out of it, and the big car went on, gradually gathering speed.

For a moment The Thunderbolt stood in the darkness at the edge of the woods. In one hand he held a bottle he had taken from the roadster— a bottle containing kerosene. Under the other arm was the bundle of bonds.

He went into the woods for a short distance, until he came to a clear space. There he stripped off the thin black coat and trousers, put them into a pile, and added his gloves and the hood of The Thunderbolt. He emptied the bottle of kerosene over the pile, and then stood up and sighed as he donned his dress coat.

This was to be the death of The Thunderbolt. His work was at an end. John Flatchley regretted it a little. It had been adventure and excitement. But he had done it for a good reason, and not for love of stealing. He was not a criminal at heart. And there were other things in the future.

He stooped and touched a match to the pile, watched the flame start, and then darted quickly through the woods. Behind him the fire burned merrily.

When he came within sight of the club he stopped at the edge of the woods. There, beneath a heap of brush, he buried the sack of bonds. He could get them easily some day while playing golf, some day in the near future, when it would be safe.

Keeping to the shadows, he left the edge of the woods and finally gained the dark end of the veranda and drew himself over the railing. Stooping, he dusted off his pumps with a handkerchief, brushed back his heavy hair with his hands, and stepped through a French window into the lounging room, stifling a yawn, looking very much the bored man of society.

He began watching a card game, but a page called him to the telephone.

John Flatchley wondered what the call might be, but he half suspected.

"Hello!" he called.

"Is this Mr. John Flatchley?"

"Yes."

"Mr. Flatchley, I just wanted to say that——"

The conversation ended abruptly, and Flatchley grinned as he replaced the receiver on its hook. He had recognized the voice of Detective Martin Radner. He knew that Radner had ascertained that he was supposed to be at the country club, and had telephoned to see whether he was there. So much for Radner! John Flatchley wanted Radner to convince himself that The Thunderbolt could not have been John Flatchley.

And Radner was convinced when the man who had shadowed Flatchley to the club reported later that night.

"He went right to the club and he stayed there," the man said. "I was where I could watch his limousine and the front door both. He never left the building. Once I got close enough to look inside, and I saw him talking to some other men in the big room with all the leather chairs in it."

"I suppose I was mistaken," Radner admitted. "But I'd have bet a roll that The Thunderbolt was Flatchley."

After the telephone call John Flatchley went to the ballroom and found Agnes Larimer.

"John, you did it?" she whispered as they danced.

"I did, and successfully," he replied.

"And it is the last?"

"Yes."

"And now——"

John Flatchley held her a little closer than the dance demanded.

Later, returning to town in the limousine, she crept into his arms and snuggled there.

"I was so afraid for you," she said. "Please never turn criminal in earnest, John, if you are going to marry me. I am afraid that I couldn't stand it. The anxiety would kill me. Criminals' wives must suffer a lot!"

"I suppose they do," Flatchley said. "But let's forget all about it. How about a month from to-day?"

"What do you mean, John?"

"Suppose," said Flatchley, "that we give some hard-working preacher a job a month from to-day."

"If you'll agree, we'll make it a month from yesterday," she said. "It's past midnight now. And it will be a sort of—anniversary."

John Flatchley's reply was not in words.

It would not do, of course, to forget faithful and loyal Mr. Saggs. When John Flatchley returned to his suite an hour or so later, Saggs opened the door for him. Flatchley looked at him questioningly.

"It was a cinch, boss," Saggs said. "I turned in the roadster and told the garage man she was all right except there was a squeak in one spring. Then I got into the house the same way I left it. The dicks were still watching in the street and alley, but about an hour ago they left. Got a tip, I suppose, that there wasn't any more use watchin'."

"I imagine that's it, Saggs."

"You got the stuff?"

"A little more than a hundred thousand, Saggs."

"And now we're—we're done?" Saggs asked.

"We are, Saggs. Henceforth we are law-abiding citizens. The Thunderbolt has ceased to exist."

Saggs looked down at the floor and kicked one foot against the other.

"Well, we've had a great time!" he announced.

"Saggs!"

"Well, boss?"

"Notice any change taking place in me? No? Well, I am changing, Saggs. Ah! I no longer am The Thunderbolt—now I am John Flatchley, forever and ever. Amen!"

Saggs gulped. "Yes, sir," he said. "What time do you wish to be called in the morning, sir?"

THE END

www.ingramcontent.com/pod-product-compliance
Lightning Source LLC
Chambersburg PA
CBHW010805250626
47156CB00010B/3006